NO ESCAPE

By Sarah Kemp

NO ESCAPE
OVER THE EDGE

NO ESCAPE

SARAH KEMP

ASBURY PARK PUBLIC LIBRARY
ASBURY PARK, NEW JERSEY

PUBLISHED FOR THE CRIME CLUB BY
DOUBLEDAY & COMPANY, INC.
GARDEN CITY, NEW YORK
1984

All of the characters in this book
are fictitious, and any resemblance
to actual persons, living or dead,
is purely coincidental.

ASBURY PARK PUBLIC LIBRARY
ASBURY PARK, NEW JERSEY

Library of Congress Cataloging in Publication Data
    No escape.
    I. Title.
PR6052.U9N6   1984   823'.914
ISBN 0-385-19331-9
Library of Congress Catalog Card Number 83–16475
Copyright © 1984 by Sarah Kemp
All Rights Reserved
Printed in the United States of America
First Edition

NO ESCAPE

ONE

It is a hard life, being on the run. Especially for a woman. A man may doss where he can find a warm place: a climb over park railings will present him with a rich choice of benches and shelters where he may sleep, and in lieu of blankets there are newspapers in abundance to be had from trash bins. If all else fails and the weather is foul, a few coppers will buy him a rough bed and a blanket in a doss house or a Salvation Army hostel.

For a woman, it is quite different. To live rough, a woman must be nearly born to it, and the young woman with green eyes certainly did not possess that expertise. She feared hostels because she had heard somewhere that these are the first places where the police look when they are after someone, so her solution was to find work, by which she could earn sufficient to get a room in the cheapest possible private lodging house. That was the important thing: a roof over her head and a door to bolt against the world. If there was anything left over for food, so much the better—but food was of secondary importance.

After Easter of that year, she found herself in Westhampton, where she saw in a tobacconist's window a card advertising a job as "finisher" in a workshop producing lampshades for the wholesale trade.

The workshop was run by a stout woman who wore heavy brass bangles and a man's wristwatch on her ham-like arms. Her eyes, sunk in rolls of flesh, were malevolently watchful.

"I'm Mrs. Beverstock. What's your name?" she demanded.

"Eileen Porter. Er—Miss Eileen Porter."

"Live around here?"

"I—I shall be looking for digs at lunchtime."

The woman grunted, her gaze taking in the other's down-at-heel shoes, the undarned cuffs of her cardigan, and—notwithstanding—the clean hair and well-tended fingernails.

"Don't s'pose you've got an employment card?"

"No—I haven't worked before." It was a formula she always used.

The woman was satisfied. "The work's casual, wages by results. Five pence a piece, take it or leave it. No insurance stamps. No questions. A minute's notice both ways. Are you going or staying?"

"I'll stay," said Eileen Porter.

The work was simple, but tedious and repetitious. She was given, by a spavined youth with a squint, a tall pile of metal lampshade frames to which she was to sew plastic panels. Afterwards she had to finish them off with a row of fringe round the bottom. By midmorning, she had completed three: fifteen pence in an hour and a half. She wouldn't get very fat on that—not unless she improved her time. Trouble was, she never seemed able to stay long enough in any one place to become good at anything.

The spavined youth came down to the cellar workshop at eleven with a mug of tea for her.

"That'll be six pence, love," he said. "Biscuit extra. Call it ten pence." He winked.

"I'll do without the biscuit," she said. A cup of hot sweet tea would serve her for lunch.

"You can have the biscuit thrown in with the six pence," he said. "I was only trying it on."

Despite herself, she laughed. "You've got the cheek of Lambley Jack," she declared.

"Lambley Jack? Who's he when he's at home?"

Mrs. Beverstock wore carpet slippers around the place, but she still had a heavy tread on the stair. They looked round as she called out.

"Lambley Jack? It's many a long year since I heard that name, and don't ask me who he was, 'cos I don't believe he even existed. But I know where *you* come from all right, young lady."

"I—I'm afraid I don't . . ." faltered the woman with green eyes.

"From Nottingham," declared Mrs. Beverstock. "My mother was from Nottingham and I remember her always saying that my dad had the cheek of Lambley Jack. She lived in the Radford district, did my mother. Where did you live? Not Radford—that'd be too much of a coincidence." Her voice was almost amiable.

"I—I don't know," whispered Eileen Porter.

"Don't know? Don't *know?*" The watchful eyes became affronted.

"I mean, I—I can't remember."

(Oh, God, she'd said the wrong thing. It was about time she learned to lie. Why hadn't she said, "I was only a kiddie when my family left Nottingham"? But it was too late now.)

Mrs. Beverstock snorted. "Well, I should think anybody who couldn't remember where they used to live ought to go and have their head looked at!" Transferring her easily aroused spleen to the grinning youth, she said, "And you can get about your work, you cheeky devil! I don't slave and worry to keep layabout cripples in idleness!" She pounded upstairs, driving the youth before her, lashed on by her tongue.

Alone again, Eileen Porter buried her face in her trembling hands. She'd done it again. Only one thing to do now.

But she must have money. Enough, at least, to buy herself a seat in the cinema, where she could sleep till they closed, and leave her rested, so she could walk around after nightfall and keep out of the way of the police.

If only she dare ask that old woman for the fifteen pence she owed her—that would help a bit.

An hour or so later, Mrs. Beverstock came downstairs again, to find the three finished lampshades still lying on the worktable. The door into the area was ajar and so was that of the outside lavatory, which was empty.

"Gone!" exclaimed the woman. "She was a funny un and no mistake! Gave me the creeps, she did!"

She tramped back upstairs to finish her last cup of tea of the morning—which, incidentally, was also the last cup of tea of her life.

TWO

St. Paul's was chiming the quarter hour when Jeremy Cook came out of the Barristers' Robing Room. He passed an old friend and fellow ex-pupil on the staircase and they fixed up a game of squash that evening at seven.

The long lobby outside the courtrooms was full of the usual cluster of counsel and solicitors, clients, witnesses, ushers—it looked like the anteroom of a sedately dressed hell, save for one youth in a studded black leather jacket and hair in a yellow-dyed Mohican. There was also a quite strikingly attractive girl in a tweed suit with a Hermès scarf knotted loosely at the throat. She was ash blonde, tall, and carried herself with an air of elegant assurance. She appeared to be searching for someone—or something.

"Can I help you?" asked Cook, sidling up to her and letting her have the full advantage of his superior height, plus the best smile he could crinkle—the one he habitually saved for susceptible lady witnesses of uncertain years.

"How kind of you." She had the voice that went with the looks: cool, very smart, assured. "Actually, I'm looking for Number One Court."

"That one over there," said Cook, pointing. "But I wouldn't advise it if I were you."

"And why's that?" she asked, amused.

"Nasty case," he said. "Most unpleasant details." A self-confessed master at docketing people, he put her down as a ladies' magazine journalist on the prowl for "local colour." Many such of the Fourth Estate haunted the Old Bailey, and the current Fawcett case in One would certainly attract the ghouls. "Besides," he added, "I doubt if you'll find room in there."

"Mr. Cook, Mr. Cook! Thank 'eavens I've found you!" The newcomer was clerk to a solicitor for whose client he would be acting the following day. His difficulties being quickly sorted out, Cook turned to readdress the fascinating blonde—and found her gone.

With a slight sense of deprivation, he made his way into Number One Court and took his place beside his Leader, Marcus Struthers, Q.C. A quick look behind him to the crowded public gallery and another swift pan of the press box elicited the sad fact that she was not present.

The jury having been sworn in, Marcus Struthers rose to outline the case for the prosecution. The accused, Gerald Norman Fawcett, he told the court, was aged forty-two, an unemployed weighing machine salesman whose common-law wife had, till the previous September, been employed as principal buyer in the women's fashion department at Messrs. Handley, Fogg & Whipple of Oxford Street, W.1., under the name of Mrs. Eileen Fawcett.

On September 7 of the previous year, continued the prosecutor, the accused was seen to drive his common-law wife from the home they shared in Great Dunmow, ostensibly to the railway station at Audley End, on the first stage of her journey, via Liverpool Street Station, London, to Heathrow Airport and a flight to a fortnight's holiday alone in Spain.

"M'lud," said Mr. Struthers, "Mrs. Fawcett was never seen alive again!" Allowing the declaration to hang in the air for a few moments to achieve maximum effect, he went on to tell how evidence would be produced to prove that the woman had not left the country either by air or by sea on the material dates—or since. Mr. Fawcett, moreover, when his common-law wife did not return from the alleged Span-

ish holiday, told friends and neighbours that Mrs. Fawcett
was staying with her mother, and at about Christmas, when
she still did not return, said that they had agreed to an
amicable separation.

Evidence would be forthcoming, continued Struthers,
with the air of a practiced carpenter knocking the few last
nails into a coffin lid, that the total balance of £7,000.50 in
Mrs. Fawcett's personal deposit account was withdrawn—
by her signature—on September 10 of the previous year—
three days after she was seen for the last time.

All eyes, by this part of the peroration, had shifted by
uneasy stages to the figure in the dock. The accused prisoner, an undersized greying man in a crumpled navy blue
suit, no collar and tie, with secret eyes shielded behind pebble glasses, was looking down at his hands.

Struthers adjusted his neat grey horsehair wig, hitched up
his silk gown more firmly across his shoulders, and resumed. "There the matter rested," he said, "till March
twelfth of this year, when, due to the activity of certain local
cats, added to complaints from users of the coin-operated
luggage lockers at Liverpool Street Station, locker number
18 was forced open. Inside, contained within a cheap fibre
suitcase, was found—and in an advanced state of decomposition—the naked, headless, and dismembered torso of a
woman in the prime of life." It was the Crown's case, said
the prosecutor, his preamble drawing to a close, that this
was the torso of the murdered Mrs. Fawcett, placed there
by her common-law spouse—after beheading and dismemberment to preclude identity—and that evidence would be
produced to prove this charge beyond all reasonable doubt.

Supportive evidence in the case of *Regina* v. *Fawcett* began
with the testimony of the police constable who was present
at the opening of locker number 18 on the day in question.
Next came a police surgeon, who attested that there were no

distinguishing marks on the torso save an old scar that must have dated back a decade or more and was evidence of an appendectomy.

Defending Counsel rose. "Is not an appendectomy one of the most common of all abdominal operations?" he enquired.

"Yes, sir. I—I suppose it must be."

"What is the incidence of appendectomies per head of population in Britain?"

"Um—I—I'm afraid I don't have the figures with me at the moment," replied the unhappy medic.

"Thank you, Doctor," said counsel with a note of finality.

"I—I'm very sorry, but, you see . . ."

"That will be all, Doctor." Counsel sat down.

So in one stroke were both the credibility and, by implication, the competence of the police surgeon called to question. Everyone in the courtroom with an appendectomy scar (like those who, similarly scarred, would be reading the day's proceedings in the *Evening Courier)* would regard it as a very poor proof of specific identity, unless supported by something like—well—birthmarks for starters, prominent moles, injury scars, even tattoos at a long shot. And no such corroboration appeared to be forthcoming.

As Counsel for the Defence remarked to his instructing solicitor, *sotto voce,* Marcus Struthers had nothing but circumstantial evidence to support the Crown's case.

"Do you have any further witnesses who might conveniently be heard before the luncheon recess, Mr. Struthers?" asked Mr. Justice Hatchett.

"M'lud, I should like to call the Home Office pathologist, Dr. J. A. Kettle," responded Struthers.

"Kettle—hmmm!" The learned judge was well known for his aversion to "expert witnesses" and in particular to the eminent forensic scientist in question, who had achieved a considerable popular TV following for his gruesomely illustrated demonstrations. It was jolly, avuncular Dr. J. A. Kettle, with his cosy fireside manner, who proved that evisceration could be laughed off with a pun and the tangible proof of mortality made to simulate a warm sense of well-being in the healthy and alive.

"Unfortunately, m'lud, Dr. Kettle is indisposed," continued Struthers. "I am informed, however, that his assistant Dr. T. P. May is present and will give evidence."

"Call him, then. Call him!" barked Mr. Justice Hatchett, with a glance at the clock. "I shall certainly adjourn for luncheon at twelve-thirty."

Dr. T. P. May was called. Struthers leaned over towards his Junior. "Jeremy, I must go," he murmured. "You handle this guy. Try and stretch it out till luncheon and beyond if you can. See you this afternoon."

He got up, bowed to the judge, and left the court. On the way out, he stood aside to allow the passage of a tall blonde, who walked sedately to the witness box, where she took the Bible in her right hand, and before Jeremy Cook's astonished gaze, read aloud the words on the card. Entirely composed, she then glanced coolly round the court.

"Pray proceed with your examination of the witness, Mr. —er—Cook, is it?" said the judge.

"Yes, m'lud. I'm much obliged." Jeremy got to his feet, brief in hand, and addressed the striking creature in the witness box.

"Um, Dr. May, your full name is . . ."

"Tina Patricia May," she supplied. "Of 18 Lochiel Street, Chelsea, South-West Three."

"Please state your professional qualifications in brief, Dr. May," he said.

"I graduated as Doctor of Medicine from All Hallows' Hospital Medical School," came the response. "Hanley-Parker Gold Medallist in Bacteriology, Grenville Prizeman, Sutton Scholar, and Van Dyke Waterlow Student."

"Have you published, Doctor?"

"Yes. *The Future of Forensic Medicine,* which was awarded the Morley Hammond Prize. And I am at present collaborating with a treatise on violent crime with Dr. Kettle, whose assistant I am."

"You are giving evidence on behalf of Dr. Kettle," said Jeremy Cook, "who carried out an autopsy upon the remains for the Home Office?"

"That is so," responded Tina May.

"Would you be so kind as to give the court a résumé of Dr. Kettle's findings, please."

Tina May took from her shoulder bag a sheaf of typescript, and placing a pair of glasses on the bridge of her very straight nose, gave her evidence, referring only occasionally to the script.

"Dr. Kettle performed the autopsy on the thirteenth of last month," she began, "and I was present at that time. The remains, the female torso, was in an advanced state of decomposition, but it was possible to determine that the cause of death was barbiturate poisoning hastened by manual strangulation. Traces of a large overdose of secobarbital, an active ingredient of preparations commonly referred to as 'sleeping pills,' was found to be present in conjunction with an amount of whisky. Traces of bruising and abrasions consistent with manual strangulation were present on the stump of the neck, below the point of severance of the head.

"The beheading and dismemberment were carried out from between three to five hours after death and before the onset of rigor mortis. This—the operation—was performed by a person or persons with no anatomical knowledge, inasmuch as the limbs and neck, instead of having been sliced through quite easily at the large articulations, were butchered with a chopper and a blunt hacksaw—with considerable difficulty." She paused and took out a sheaf of colour transparencies. "I have a set of photos taken of the trunk with the viscera displayed," she said, removing her glasses. "Though of considerable interest in the canon of morbid pathology, the layman may find them disturbing to view. It must be remembered that it was only with considerable difficulty that one was able to remove the remains from the suitcase in one piece . . ."

"Enter the photographs as evidence," said the judge stoutly, "and show them to the jury."

A hush fell upon the courtroom as the photos were passed from Dr. May to the usher, and from the usher to the foreman of the jury.

In the continuing silence, the foreman lifted the upper print so that he could view it against the afternoon light that streamed in from the high window at the opposite side of the chamber.

Those who were able to see his face remarked afterwards that it grew suddenly pale and that his massive jaw fell open. Certainly everyone in Number One Court saw the prints fall from his suddenly nerveless hands as, without a murmur, he slipped quietly to his knees and fell prone.

Mr. Justice Hatchett cleared his throat. "Hem! I think this will be as good a time as any to recess for luncheon."

The truck driver was twenty-eight years of age and strongly built. Midway from elbow to wrist of his right forearm there was a tattoo of a pair of clasped hands with the legend underneath: *Friendship*. The arms, like most of his body, were covered with a pelt of sandy hair. He had a bland, expressionless face set with small eyes of indeterminate colour somewhere between hazel and grey.

Clear of Westhampton, a wind got up, and with it a flurry of rain. Away to his right, from the direction of the Cotswold Hills, there came a slow drum roll of distant thunder.

He slowed at an intersection, by a signpost pointing the way he was going. It read: *Motorway M1 – London 53 miles.*

The figure of a young woman in a cardigan and jeans stood forlornly by the post. At the sight of her, he applied the brakes, and with a gusting of air the giant articulated truck drew to a halt.

He poked his head out of the cab window. "Wanna lift?"

She nodded eagerly.

"Hop in, then."

It was a long way up to the cab, but his powerful right arm hoisted her as if she had been a doll. Close up, he saw that she had a nice body—though a bit on the skinny side—and very clear green eyes. He'd picked up worse in his time.

"Goin' to London?" he asked.

She nodded.

"Right—that makes the pair of us. Ciggie?" He held out a packet.

"No, thanks. I don't smoke."

He released the hand brake and gunned the big diesel engine.

" 'Spect you've been listening to all that stuff about ciggies giving you cancer," he said. "It's stupid. Why, it stands to sense. My old dad, he smoked like a chimney all his life and never had a day's illness. He'd be alive now, only he fell under a bus." The recollection amused him.

"I couldn't afford to anyhow," she said. And immediately looked away.

"A bit up against it, then, are you?" he asked, glancing at her sidelong. And when she did not answer: "Going after a job in London, are you?"

She nodded.

"What's your line?"

"Oh—mostly anything."

"Casual like, eh? Got your insurance cards stamped up?"

She shook her head.

"Just come out of prison, have you?" As far as he was

concerned, this was the only category of folks who did not possess National Insurance cards, duly stamped up to date.

"No!" she cried.

"All right, all right," he said, grinning. "Don't bite me head off. You could find it a bit difficult getting a job—a decent job—unless you had the proper papers."

She did not reply.

"Of course there's no problem with cards," said her new friend after a while. "It's big business, selling 'em to foreigners who aren't supposed to be in the country anyhow. A forged one would see you through for a month or so, till they find out that the serial number's faked. The best ones used to belong to dead folks—they're good for life." He laughed.

They came to the entrance to the London-bound motorway, and she did not speak till he had negotiated the roundabout and the ramp down into the main stream of south-seeking traffic.

Later, above the hum of the tyres and the boom of the engine, she asked, "Where do you go to get these cards?"

"Interested, are you?" He looked at her again. "Well, you want to try the transport cafes" (he pronounced it "kayfs") "on the North Circular Road, Finchley and all round there. Just go in, order a mug of tea and a bun, get talking to one of the lads and bring the subject round to it. I won't say you'll score first off, but you'll make it sooner or later."

Further discourse was precluded by a teeming downpour of rain which followed a flash of lightning and a crash of thunder right overhead. Despite the frenzied motion of the windscreen wipers, inside the cab it was like looking out at the world through the sides of a goldfish bowl; to meadows where patient cattle lay in the streaming torrent, and tall soaked trees shimmered in dark woods.

Presently, when it had let up a little, she asked, "How much are they, these cards?"

"Depends," he replied. "The forged ones you can pick up for a pound or two. The good stuff, the flash stuff—why, one of them could set you back fifteen, twenty pounds."

"Oh," she said. And again: "Oh."

The rain persisted in the way that told it was going to remain like that all day. He sat hunched at the wheel, a cigarette dangling out of a corner of his mouth most of the time, intent upon keeping his safe distances from the stuff in front, in pulling out and overtaking when the moment was propitious, pulling in again with devastating expertise.

The damp heat of the cab must have made her heavy-eyed and sleepy. She did not respond at once when he next addressed her.

"Sorry—what did you say?" she asked.

"I said: Fancy a bite to eat? Got some sandwiches and a pork pie in the back here." "The back here" was a bunk and a set of shelves like a chest of drawers, all revealed by a pulled-back curtain. He had a tiny flatlet up there behind the seats.

"Well, I never had any lunch," she said.

Nor I bet you didn't have any supper last night, either, he thought. Yes, you're in there all right, Jim lad. I reckon you're going to have this little Judy for a sandwich and a bit o' pie.

"Right—we eat," he said, and flicked a switch that worked the winkers. Ahead was an exit road. Minutes later, they were in a lonely country lane, where low branches of trees wetly swept the top of the lorry in passing.

"Here's a nice spot," he said, and pulled into a lay-by off the road that was half shielded by a low hedge and drooping branches. He snicked on the brake, switched off the engine, and grinned across at her.

She looked a bit scared, but that could only be for show. He knew her sort from long experience on the roads: semi-virgins who made a bit of a pretence about keeping their

ha'penny to themselves. A pushover for smart operators like
him . . .

He rummaged behind him. There was a small cupboard
up there—a miniature larder. Also a tiny fridge.

"Like a cheese sandwich to start with?" he asked.

She nodded, and took the sandwich in one hand; with the
other she carefully held together the edges of her damp
cardigan, right up to the neck. He was familiar with the
gesture: it fitted in with his summation of her character.

He took a bite of his sandwich and eyed her covertly.
"You a bit worried about not having the dough to buy yourself a card?" he asked, chewing the while.

"Mmmm." She nodded, but absently, as if she did not
want to be questioned any more closely.

"No need to worry. Pretty girl like you can always raise a
pound or two without having to scrub floors for it." Let her
think on that. To soften the implication of his remark, he
added, "Like a drop of tea?" He produced a thermos flask
and two enamel mugs.

His crack about raising money without having to scrub
floors had obviously got under her guard—or so he reckoned from the way she withdrew from him even further.
Playing hard to get—he knew the style. Or maybe she was
just plain nervy. Anyhow, the time had come to try her. In
the event, it was she who gave him the lead:

"How long will it take to get to London from here?" she
asked.

"Oh, not long. About three quarters of an hour," he replied. "We'll set off again as soon as we've finished eating
and had a bit of a rest."

"A—a *rest?*"

"I've been driving ever since I got up this morning," he
said, "and I've got to go through London and on to Dover.
They don't allow us to do more than so many hours at a

stretch, and there's a machine in the cab that squeals on me if I cheat the time sheet. Another sandwich?"

She shook her head. "No, thanks. I'd better go if you're going to rest. Get myself another lift on the motorway."

He grinned. "What's your hurry? Plenty of room up there for two." Jerking his thumb towards the bunk behind them.

She put down her mug. "Well, thanks for the lift and everything," she said. " 'Bye for now."

Her hand was on the door catch, but he forestalled her: his hand was there first and snapping shut the locking device.

"What's your hurry, kiddo? We've got all the time in the world." His arm was round her shoulders. "Hey, you're all wet. Take off that woolly and we'll dry it against the cab heater. C'mon, you can borrow my windcheater till it's dry."

He began to peel off her cardigan. And though she kept her arms folded across her breasts and was eyeing him with something that might have been defiance, he persisted. In the end, he removed the garment, leaving her in a sleeveless cotton shirt. She huddled in the corner of the bench seat, watching him inscrutably as he made a great play of laying the damp woolly against the grille of the cab heater. Almost immediately, it began to emit a plume of steam.

He grinned at her. So far, so good. What he took to be a token show of resistance had served further to inflame him. He edged his way over to her and, avoiding her eyes—so as not to alarm her with what she might see in his—he began to unbutton her shirt, starting at the throat.

"Don't do that!" she whispered. "Just you don't do that!"

"Aw, c'mon, kiddo. Don't play hard to get any longer. Let's have a little fun. C'mon—show me what you've got in there."

For answer, she pushed his hand away and scrabbled for

the door lock. He retaliated by ripping open her shirt from neck to waist, buttons and all.

"Let me go!" she screamed.

"You little bitch!" Now he was fighting with her. "Don't come that line with me."

He had his hands on her shoulders and was forcing her round to face him. Maybe, he told himself, he'd give her a couple of sharp belts across the mouth—that often quietened them down when they thought themselves into a state of hysteria. He liked the idea. And she looked pretty good: it was with reluctance that he dragged his gaze from her gaping shirtfront to her face.

What he saw there—in her face, in the bared-teeth set of her mouth, but most of all in the flare of her wide, green eyes—quenched every desire within him and left only the cold grey edge of a nameless fear.

Instinctively, his hands came up to protect his face, but she was quicker.

He heard himself scream like a pig when she raked his face with her nails—the long, decently kept fingernails that, apart from her clean and well-brushed hair, were the only tokens that set her apart from the run of little scrubbers he usually picked up on his journeys, and who paid for their transportation in the narrow bunk above.

Before he could make the slightest attempt to check her, the sharply armed fingertips dug into the soft surrounds of his eyes and raked the hard, slippery spheres of the eyeballs. A grotesque redness filled his vision and was gone. He felt warm blood besplatter his face as he fell back on his hunkers and opened his mouth to scream against the searing pain and atavistic panic.

He felt the chill of the outside air and a flurry of rain beat against his face and chest. The door was open. She had gone. Somehow, he half climbed, half fell out of the cab and onto a bed of last year's pine cones that littered the hard standing of the lay-by.

He got back to his feet, his clothing immediately saturated and plastered to him in the teeming torrent.

And there, careless of the trailing thorn bushes that tore at his bare arms, his neck, his cheeks and hair, he blundered into the woodland that bordered the lay-by, shrieking all the time, calling for help: help from anyone—even from her. Blundering like Samson Agonistes. Bereft. Terrified. Broken. Alone.

Blinded!

Jeremy Cook had looked out for Dr. T. P. May; had rushed out from unrobing and run both ways up and down Holborn Viaduct and Newgate Street in search of her, till he sulkily settled for a solitary luncheon at a nearby pub: a grill and half a bottle of St.-Emilion. It was still raining when he crossed back to the Old Bailey.

She was talking to Marcus Struthers when he entered the courtroom. Noticing him from the corner of her eye, she was quietly amused to see how he preened himself at the sight of her: adjusted his neckband, straightened his wig, hitched up his gown.

"Jeremy," said Struthers, "Dr. May here, who I am sure must have come as much a surprise to you as she has to me, seems to have broken the case during the luncheon recess."

"Really?" The younger man looked at her interrogatively.

"I think—no, I'm quite sure—that the remains in the locker were those of Mrs. Fawcett," she said. "I followed up a hunch and checked it out at St. Wilfred's Hospital. It's all here—" She showed them a stiff grey envelope folder.

"It's new evidence," said Struthers.

"Shouldn't we tell Jake Scott?" said his Junior.

"Jake Scott's the Counsel for the Defence," Struthers explained to her. "He isn't going to be very pleased with this setback."

"Here he comes now," said Cook.

"Too late. Here comes the judge."

"Silence in court and be upstanding!" intoned an usher. Mr. Justice Hatchett came out of a door at the back, acknowledged counsels' deep bows, took his seat beneath the Royal Coat of Arms on the high wall. "Let us continue with the evidence of Dr. May," he said, and beamed across at her in the witness box.

"No need to swear the oath again, ma'am," whispered the usher.

The foreman of the jury appeared to have recovered from his fainting fit, but in a curious way was greatly diminished in stature. Tina May looked down at her hands holding the folder and saw that they were trembling with suppressed excitement. She glanced across at Marcus Struthers, who was getting to his feet. Jeremy Cook was looking at her. Everyone was looking at her—except the accused prisoner, she noticed.

"M'lud," began Struthers, "I have to tell you that the witness has unearthed some new evidence over the recess which your lordship may well consider to satisfy the Crown's case in every respect."

"M'lud!" The defender, Jake Scott, made a great play of tired exasperation as he got up. "It seems to me that my learned friend has been watching too many court cases of the lurid kind on TV. With respect, m'lud, no one knows better than yourself that this kind of eleventh-hour submission of fresh evidence of which the defence has not been apprised simply isn't on."

"Mr. Struthers?" The judge glared at the prosecutor over his half-moon glasses.

"M'lud, the witness, as I understand, raced from this courtroom at the recess, seized a taxi, was taken to St. Wilfred's Hospital, secured the evidence, and came straight back here. There was unfortunately no time to confer with my learned friend opposite."

"M'lud," said Scott, "may I ask the court's indulgence of a short recess, so that I may examine this fresh evidence?"

The judge shifted in his chair. Tina held the folder more tightly to her side, feeling an instinctive—almost maternal —desire to keep its contents from alien hands and eyes.

"Mr. Scott," said the judge, "I am concerned to proceed with all seemly dispatch in this case. Might I propose a compromise which you will almost certainly find acceptable —namely, that the witness—the *expert* witness"—and he beamed across at her—"first be permitted to give the new evidence in open court? If you then require time to study the evidence before cross-questioning her, I shall be pleased to grant it."

It was quite obvious that Jake Scott had no alternative but to agree to the judge's "compromise suggestion." To his credit, he contrived to do it with a good grace.

And now—the moment was Tina May's . . .

"Dr. May," said Struthers. "Would you please give the court a summation of your findings as they relate to the discovery you made at St. Wilfred's during the luncheon recess."

She nodded, took from the envelope folder a sheaf of X-ray transparencies, and gave a small cough. By chance she met the eye of Jeremy Cook, then looked away quickly and began:

"In one X-ray that I took, under Dr. Kettle's direction, of the partly decomposed trunk, there appeared on the extreme upper edge of the right iliac crest of the pelvis a hairline that might have suggested an old fracture which had long since healed. But so faint was it that it did not appear on any of the other pictures, so we dismissed it as a probable fault in the X-ray plate. It was only this morning, as I was waiting outside the court to be called, that an idea occurred to me."

"And what was that, Dr. May?" asked Marcus Struthers, who knew the histrionic effect of a well-timed "feed."

"I remembered the appendectomy scar indicating a Mc-Donald's incision," she replied, consciously keeping the excited edge from her voice now that she was drawing nearer to her punchline. "This incision, I should explain, was devised by Professor Ian McDonald of St. Wilfred's Medical School, and though as a technique of entry it has never gained the popularity which it deserved, nevertheless earned a considerable éclat twenty years ago and more when it was performed at St. Wilfred's and mostly under the direction of Professor McDonald himself." She paused.

"It occurred to me," she said, "that records and X-rays of the late Professor McDonald's classic cases would almost certainly be kept at the Hospital School, where he was so venerated during the few short years—barely five years—of his appointment there, till his death. Such was the case.

"I made my wants known to the Dean of Studies, and five years of case notes and X-rays were brought to a quiet room where they had gathered together a dozen or so housemen and final-year students. I briefed them on what to look for, and we ploughed through the X-rays and notes." She paused.

"And with what result, Doctor?" asked Struthers, breaking the sepulchral silence.

For answer, Tina held up an X-ray transparency the same size as the previous one. "We found what we were looking for," she said.

"And what is that?"

"It shows the abdomen of a young girl of twenty," said Tina, "with a highly inflamed appendix due for excision. What is more, the picture also shows—by chance—the iliac crests of the patient's pelvis. And the right-hand upper edge very clearly presents a small fracture in an early stage of healing."

"And what do you deduce from your find, Dr. May?"

"That the X-ray which I took of the torso from the locker and that of Professor McDonald's patient were from the same person, separated by twenty years in time!" And now she was making no attempt to keep the excitement from her voice.

"And what, from the case records, were the name and age of Professor McDonald's patient?" asked Struthers, cocking an eye towards the jury.

"Miss Eileen Ivy Bambtree, aged nineteen," replied Tina.

There was a sudden commotion from the public gallery— as a small, bespectacled woman in a woollen hat rose to her feet and shouted, "That's right! That's my Eileen! My baby! She went to St. Wilfred's for the operation not long after she fell off the groyne at Margate and broke her hip!"

Her next declaration was delivered at the now cringing figure in the dock, and accented by her accusatory, pointing, trembling finger. "You did it, you dirty dog! You done her in for the money! May your soul rot . . ." Still screaming, she was taken by both arms and propelled from the gallery between two policemen.

By now, a posse of newspaper reporters were making a dash out to the phone booths.

Mr. Justice Hatchett miraculously made himself heard above the din: "Before that woman is evicted, will someone take her name and determine who she is?"

It was Jake Scott, Q.C., who answered him. "M'lud, she is Mrs. Bambtree, mother of the—of the murdered woman known to this court as Mrs. Eileen Fawcett."

And in that one phrase, the Counsel for the Defence conceded the case to the Crown.

The Fawcett case was truly all over bar the shouting, but Scott pleaded an adjournment till the following day in order to prepare a statement on behalf of his client, who had changed his plea to "guilty." This was granted. Upon leaving the witness box, Tina May was surrounded by reporters demanding a statement, while the features editor of *Woman's Monthly* asked if she was Taurus or Virgo and wanted to know her views on herpes and birth control.

To her relief, she was rescued by Jeremy Cook, who led her to a side door used only by court officials. Five minutes later, dressed for the street, he met her by arrangement outside Holborn Viaduct Station.

"Tea, do you think?" he asked.

"That will be nice," she said.

The newsboy at the station entrance was unregarded by them, as well as the poster on his stand, which announced:

E X T R A

DOUBLE MURDER IN
WESTHAMPTON

If they had troubled to buy a copy of the *Evening Courier,* they might have read the item:

WOMAN AND YOUTH SLAIN IN COLD BLOOD

Callers at a small wholesale fancy goods workshop in Scarletwell Street, Westhampton, were horrified to discover the mutilated bodies of Mrs. Eliza Beverstock, 54, and Mr. Harry Finch, 18, in the basement of the establishment shortly after noon today.

"INSANE INJURIES"

One of the witnesses, Mr. D. J. Wakeley, 46, a salesman, said that Mrs. Beverstock, the proprietor, was lying in a pool of blood with her throat cut in a manner that suggested the murderer must have been insane. Close by lay the body of Finch, a handyman at the workshop.

THE MOTIVE—ROBBERY?

A police spokesman announced that a search of the premises revealed an empty cashbox which was believed to have contained only a small amount of loose change.

THREE

"How did you ever come to take on a job like this?" he asked her.

Close up, his eyes were mid-blue and flecked with touches of hazel. His hair was crisply cut, butter yellow and curly, like that of a teddy bear she had owned as a child. Weight— oh, around a hundred and fifty to eighty pounds. Athletic build, especially around the shoulders. Probably done a lot of rowing and Rugby football. Would have to watch his weight when he gave all that up in middle age . . .

"I expect you're always being asked that," he said.

She smiled. The waitress came with a tray of tea, cucumber sandwiches, and fancy cakes.

Tina poured tea for them both. "Yes, I am," she admitted, "though there are now quite a few women around in the discipline."

"Not a job for everyone," he said. "Not a job for a lot of men, I fancy."

"There are worse things to face in the medical profession than poor dead bodies," she said. "I had a vocation—at least, so I thought—to be a paediatrician, but the first time I sat with a little girl of six and watched her die of meningitis, I knew I didn't have what it takes."

He sketched a distasteful gesture. "But, I mean, it must be all so—how to put it?—so unhygienic! Long-dead bodies and all."

"I take your point," she said, "but the human skeleton is a thing of curious beauty, did you know? There are a tremendous number of not very attractive-looking people walking around who are going to make quite remarkably handsome skeletons when benevolent nature has done her work."

He took another cucumber sandwich and sliced it neatly in half—as neatly, she thought, as any surgeon might have done. "You don't convince me," he said, "but I think you're wonderful, to do what you do and remain quite untouched by it all."

He was asking her more about herself, and she was disposed to tell him a certain amount, but not all . . .

"And what of your home in Chelsea. Do you live alone?"

"I share with two others," she said. "I have the ground and the garden floors. Up above is an old school friend of mine. Alice is a teacher and tremendously keen on our having a Red revolution. In the attic we have Jock, who's a writer, keeps himself to himself, and regularly gets drunk whenever he receives a cheque."

"How did you come by Jock?" he asked.

She had never made any great mystery about her relationship with Jock—not on the superficial level, at any rate. The numerous complications she habitually kept under wraps.

"Oh, Jock's my ex-husband, but he's quite clean about the house."

"Oh, I see."

"No, you don't, Mr. Cook," she responded with a touch of amused mockery, "but it doesn't matter, doesn't matter at all."

They rounded out a most enjoyable meal by ordering a pot of orange congou tea, which they discovered to be a mutual passion. They did it very well at the cafe, with tiny, delicate Chinese bowls to drink out of, and a mimosa blossom floating in a dish of scented water.

Now tell me something about you, she had demanded, and he was only too ready to oblige.

It was a conventional tale of his age and class: Rugby School and Christ Church, Oxford. Called to the Bar a year later than his parents had scheduled—and this on account of a season that he had spent in Paris, Amsterdam, and Katmandu, at which latter-day nirvana of seekers after self, he had studied at the feet of a well-known guru, been inducted as an acolyte of the fifth degree, and succumbed to a dose of hepatitis which had necessitated his return home and, eventually, back to the groves of Academe, a sadder and wiser youth.

At nearly pub-opening time, he suggested that they adjourn to a bar, and she, greatly enjoying his stories of cases he had worked on in the criminal courts, agreed. He took her to the Savoy, where they had two dry martinis apiece and she told him about her lucky association with the veteran pathologist J. A. Kettle and how the TV scientific "personality" had greatly advanced her career opportunities. Again, she dissembled slightly and did not touch upon an aspect of her relationship with Kettle that was private to them both.

At well after seven o'clock, Jeremy remembered that he had stood up his friend for a game of squash. "But it doesn't matter a bit," he said. "Jimmy will find plenty of people to play with at the club. What I would like to do, Tina" (they had slipped into first-name terms with the arrival of the second martini), "is to take you to dinner. Are you free this evening?" He eyed her with ill-concealed anxiety.

"I shall have to pop home and change," she said. "This getup, to me, seems to carry the odour of the law courts and the foetid stench of Newgate Gaol."

"I thought it was your expensive French scent," responded Jeremy. And they both laughed.

In the event, he saw her to a taxi home and it was ar-

ranged that she call him at his flat in Upper Brook Street
when she was ready. They would then meet up at Wheelers.
Before she was driven off, he squeezed her hand and pecked
her cheek; said he was looking forward to seeing her in
about an hour or so. She concurred.

Alas for happy anticipation.

She had no sooner paid off the cab and let herself in than
Alice came clattering downstairs in dressing gown and
mules, her face covered in cold cream, hair in curlers.

"Jock's gone out on a bender!" she cried.

"Is it a cheque?"

"Came on the afternoon delivery. A hundred and fifty—
he waved it in front of me and did a little Red Indian dance.
Tina, you know I'd stay and help out, but I really *am* no use
with Jock when he's been on a bender, and anyhow, I'm due
at a demo outside the Albert Hall at eight. The damn Fas-
cists are sponsoring a concert of Wagner and Richard
Strauss and we're going to make a peaceful protest." (The
last peaceful protest had landed Alice in Bow Street magistrates' court on a charge of obstruction and carrying a blunt
instrument with the intent of causing grievous bodily harm.)

"I'll hold the fort," said Tina with resignation. I'd best
ring Jeremy and tell him I've got to chuck tonight, she
thought.

"Oh, and Dr. Kettle's secretary phoned," said Alice. "It's
quite important, and will you please ring back just as soon
as you get in." She ran back up the stairs, three at a time, to
continue the task of making herself beautiful—for the benefit of the magistrates on the morrow, without a doubt.

Kettle must have been sitting close by the phone awaiting
her call: he was on the line almost immediately.

"Johnny, it's Tina," she said. "How are you?"

"I had the report on the Fawcett case," he said. "That

was a great piece of forensic detective work. Congratulations."

"And how are you?" she persisted. "You had another relapse today—right?"

"It comes and goes, Tina."

"Oh, why don't you agree to have the op?" she pleaded.

"It's too late now. It was too late right from the start. You know that."

Up above her head, in the bathroom on the next floor, Alice pulled the plug of the hand basin, and the water gurgled away along the veteran Victorian plumbing system.

She took a deep breath. "But what are you going to *do*, Johnny?"

"You know the score, my dear. I've got a year, maybe a little less, before I have to take to my bed. Till then, I'm going to squeeze the last ounce of pleasure out of everything: my work, my books, my modest collection of pictures. Friends . . ." He lingered over the last word and Tina began to cry quietly. "And then, dear Tina, I'm going to help myself out of life and go in peace. Without pain. With dignity. . . . But that wasn't why I asked you to ring me," he added in his habitual brisk, matter-of-fact tones.

"Why did you ask me to ring you?" she responded in kind, wiping her eyes with a fingertip, spilling the dam of each lower lid and letting the floods trickle down her cheeks.

"There's a double murder come up in Westhampton," he replied. "The Yard has been called to supply a pathologist, so I proposed you. Too late tonight, but get an early train up there tomorrow, will you? Ring me if you have any problems. The chap to contact is Detective Chief Superintendent Conigsby, and here's his number . . ."

Tina wrote it down.

"I'll say good night. Sleep well, and good luck in Westhampton."

She needed to say so much more; instead, she merely mumbled the conventional response and rang off.

The call to Jeremy Cook took little or no time at all. She told him that she had to go up to Westhampton right away, that evening, and the white lie did not hurt at all. And, yes, she would contact him just as she returned and they'd fix up another date.

She bathed and put on nightgown and wrapper, took up a book, and made herself comfortable on the counterpane to while away the night till Jock fell in through the door and had to be looked after. At nine o'clock, Alice came downstairs, called out, "See you," and departed to keep her tryst with the Wagner and Strauss lovers.

At half past nine, wearied with a long day that had been memorable for her first really important appearance in court, she dropped the book onto her lap. Her muzzy thoughts drifted between Johnny Kettle and Jock, glissading lightly over Jeremy Cook—till at last she fell asleep with her reading glasses still perched on the end of her elegant nose.

In the early dawn, the young woman with the green eyes rose from the shelter of a hollowed-out hole beneath a dead willow tree that overhung a stream (in fact, it was an otter's sett, the architect and late inmate having run his last race against the hunters and the hounds), stripped herself naked, and bathed in the limpid stream, afterwards drying herself in the thin morning sunlight. Scraping her comb through her hair and dressing herself again, she set off to find what she most needed: something to eat and drink.

Two fields and a copse away from the stream, a quite busy secondary road ran from a small market town to the nearest junction of the motorway to London. Commercial traffic, London-bound, started to move along the road as early as six in the morning, and the tea and coffee stall that operated in a lay-by did good business through till evening, with a bonus during the tourist season; specializing in tea and coffee, as announced, but also enjoying a roaring trade in hot dogs and burgers, sandwiches, soft drinks, ice cream, and confectionery.

At five-thirty, the owner of the stall let down the flap that opened his counter for business—and found himself face to face with his first customer of the day.

"Blimey, you're early, miss," he said. "What'll it be?"

"Tea, please," said the young woman.

He scalded a metal teapot with the contents of a water boiler and presently poured a mug of the dark amber brew. "Anything to go with it?" he asked, noticing her sidelong glance at the franks, burgers, and chopped onions sizzling companionably on the griddle.

"Er—no—no, thanks," she said. Nor did he miss the touch of wistfulness in her voice, and he immediately felt sorry for her. In his job he saw many such: young folks on the road, trudging somewhere to find work as often as not. Stony broke, all.

Eyeing her covertly over his own mug of tea, he decided he liked the look of her—she seemed straight and wholesome, clean fingernails, well-scrubbed complexion, and no slop covering up a mucky face. He decided to proceed with caution, so as not to cause offence.

"I hope you hadn't been waiting long," he said. "My regular assistant let me down yesterday, went off and got herself another job without giving notice, so I had to start the day by washing up last night's dishes. I hate washing up. How does it grab *you?*"

She shrugged. "It's got to be done," she said.

After a moment, he said, "If you should happen to be searching for a job, this one's going."

She met his eye and looked away.

"One pound fifty an hour," he said.

She was tapping the side of her mug.

"Meals thrown in," he said. "Including breakfast."

She nodded, and her eyes swivelled back to the griddle again, from which wafted the heady scent of chopped onions going slightly brown in the sizzling fat.

"All right," she said.

I reckon it was the thought of a square meal that did it, he told himself. One thing, it's not because of my pretty face and the way I tie my tie, that's for sure. She's not that kind of kid anyhow—you can tell that at a glance. A real nice girl—the sort you could take home and show Mum.

"There's an apron in the locker," he said. "You'd better serve yourself breakfast before the customers start arriving in large lumps. And you can fix me another mug of tea if you will."

"All right," she said.

"What's your name?" he asked.

"Um—Ruth."

"All right, Ruth. I'm Norman," he said.

The Westhampton murders screamed from the front pages of the tabloids and occupied prestigious places in the quality dailies. Tina bought a selection of both sorts to read on the train. The bald outline of the double slaying had not been greatly expanded from the account—which she had not seen—of the previous evening, save that the police were seeking to interview a young woman who was believed to have visited the workshop on the morning of the crime.

She scanned the stories and was mildly amused to observe the familiar phenomenon of disparity among the reports: Mrs. Beverstock, the murdered woman, was variously described as being fifty-two, fifty-four, and "early sixties"; both widowed and separated from her husband. The youth Finch was said to have been a victim of polio in one account and multiple sclerosis in all the others; but there was a unanimity regarding his age, eighteen. Detective Chief Superintendent Conigsby—the officer whom she was due to contact on arrival—was in charge of the enquiries, they said.

She sat back in her seat and closed her eyes, still tired, despite an untroubled night. Jock had never come home, which meant that the bender was going to be of an exceptionally protracted sort. Alice had arrived home quite early and was still fast asleep when she had left—it being still the school Easter holidays. She had thought to ring Johnny Kettle before she came out, but dismissed the idea. He might have suffered a pain-racked night and still be sleeping.

She was contemplating the latter image when the train pulled into the Westhampton station.

Alec Conigsby had had his plainclothesmen in for a briefing and out on the streets by nine o'clock that morning. The bodies of the murdered pair had been photographed *in situ*, both floors of the workshop gone over with a fine comb, everything in sight fingerprinted twice over, descriptions of the strange girl sent to all police authorities, the press and TV. It had finally been established that Mr. Richard Evan Beverstock, husband of the murdered woman, had recently died in a YMCA hostel after having been parted from his spouse for ten years. She had no other living relatives. Finch, who had been raised in an orphanage, had no one who was remotely interested in his passing.

Both bodies had been dispatched to the mortuary. He now waited for the messengers whom he had sent out into the morning air to come back with the answers.

Conigsby had just taken from a box in his drawer a sugared almond—his great weakness—when the voice of his assistant, Detective Sergeant Grant, came over the intercom: "Dr. May phoning from the station, sir."

"Tell her to wait there. Tell her to get herself a cup of

coffee in the buffet. I'll be over to take her straight to the mortuary. Order my car, Frank."

They had told him that the pathologist was a woman, but had not mentioned that she was an absolute smasher. At the first sight of the one and only person in the station buffet, Conigsby had a feeling that he should have straightened his tie, smoothed back his hair, cleaned his shoes, and put on a better suit.

On the way to the mortuary, he briefed her: "The motive had to be robbery, though there couldn't have been more than a few pounds in the cashbox. I don't know how it will strike you, Doctor, but for my money, whoever killed that pair must be sick in the mind. To do what she did to that couple for a handful of loose change! Mind you, it could have been out of spite for there being so little cash."

"You said, 'she,' " commented Tina. "I suppose you're referring to the young woman mentioned in the papers."

"She's all we have to go on right now," replied the other, "and I've got around to thinking of the killer as a she."

"How did you get on to her?"

"Easiest thing in the world. The proprietor of the tobacconist's shop saw her looking at the small ads on postcards in the window. He saw her copying down the address from the card that had to be Mrs. Beverstock's. He was able to give us a description."

"A good description?"

"There are no good descriptions, Doctor. What we have would fit half the young women in the West Midlands. Only one item is worth tuppence: she was wearing a light blue cardigan with a pattern of dark-coloured diamond shapes round the waist. Of course, we've omitted that from the circularized description."

"Why?" asked Tina.

He glanced at her with something of the look that some

men give to women drivers. "So she won't stop wearing it out in the streets," he explained.

"Of course." She felt a fool.

They came to the mortuary, which lay behind a high wall overtopped with spikes: it was a low, square building with large frosted-glass skylights. Inside was institutional grey and green. It stank of an amalgam of formaldehyde and carbolic soap. Grant was already there waiting for them. The susceptible young detective sergeant coloured up most becomingly when his chief introduced him to Tina, who offered him her hand.

"There's a washroom-cum-changing room," said Conigsby. "It's men only, but you can bolt the door from the inside." He hefted her holdall into a bare, whitewashed vault of a place and left her. Tina stripped and put on a white clinical coat and rubber gloves, pressing her crisp blonde curls under a surgeon's cap. From her holdall she then took her instrument case and checked it over, along with notebook and clipboard, pen and coloured pencils. Not for the first time she longed for the day when she would have attained sufficient eminence to justify the salary of an assistant, or even a secretary, to take notes while she worked.

"Here we go," she said aloud. "The first murder case I've had that's all my own." She unbolted the door and went out.

They went to a cafe down the road for a cup of coffee after the autopsy. Young Grant was looking decidedly peaky, having stayed to watch against his better judgement. His whole approach and attitude to Tina May had undergone a curious metamorphosis during the last hour and a half. The vision of this cool, antiseptic vision in white squaring up to the two grotesquely contorted and ill-assorted naked corpses on the marble-topped tables would long remain

with him. The opening gambit, when she calmly sliced open
the dead woman from throat to groin, allowing the viscera
to spill out like many-coloured jujubes, was destined to
haunt his dreams.

And her running commentary—what you might call her
"patter"! . . . "The knife slash in the abdomen, you see?
That would have caused death on its own. The liver's lacerated terribly badly. . . . The cuts on the palms of the
hands, they're classic wounds of self-protection. Can you
help me turn it over, please? . . . Damn this rigor mortis,
it makes manipulation so difficult. Oh, now you've got
blood all over your trousers, I'm so sorry. . . . The blood
in the lungs, that was breathed in after the throat was cut
. . . a nasty cut. . . . I quite agree with you, Chief Superintendent, insane frenzy directed that cut. See how it's been
repeated at the back of the neck, as if the killer had a notion
at first to sever the head? . . . Not much else to see as
regards the wounds on the woman. . . . I'll examine the
other body, then remove the vital organs for lab examination. . . . Yes, one must never overlook the possibility of
poison, though it hardly seems likely in these two cases.
. . . Well, here we go with Number Two. Poor youngster,
it was polio after all . . . must have contracted it in early
childhood. Whatever drove the killer to attack the eyes?
. . . Some homicidal psychopaths have a fixation about
eyes, you know . . ."

So it had gone on, with horror piled upon horror, for that
whole hour and a half, during which time the principal ac-
tor didn't falter once in her lines or actions and he, witness
to his first postmortem examination, kept on his feet and
halfway to sanity by what could only have been a triumph
of mind over matter. As for the chief, though he kept a
straight face and never hesitated to step forward and give
the lady a hand, he had never looked so peaky, and drank
his coffee with the air of a man who wished it was neat

scotch. In this he was right, for Conigsby, though it had been far from his first postmortem, had found that the spectacle of a beautiful woman as principal performer added something of the bizarre. And he found himself no longer regarding Tina May with the leery attitude with which some men have towards women drivers. Indeed, he deferred to her.

"What do you think, then, Doctor?" he asked. "Is it a straight knife job?"

"Almost certainly," she responded. "The sort of person who kills for small gains would scarcely complicate matters by resorting to narcotics as a preliminary, as I fancy the laboratory examination of the organs will establish. No, I don't see our culprit slipping a barbiturate into the victims' tea in order to get them in a soporific state for the killings."

Conigsby grunted. "There were two unwashed teacups in the ground-floor kitchen sink," he said. "Neither bore traces of any kind of drug, the police lab tells us."

Tina nodded.

"There was a third cup in the downstairs workroom," he added. "Left there half finished."

"By the mystery girl, you think?"

"That's for sure. We got a full set of fingerprints from it."

"Known fingerprints?"

He looked disappointed. "No. But we'll know her next time—if she's moved into regular business."

"If you can spare me a corner of your office and a typewriter, Mr. Conigsby," she said, "I'll make out my preliminary report before I set off back to London. I take it," she added, "that you'll not be requiring me any more at this time."

"Not till the trial," he said with a tight-lipped grin. "When we catch her—as catch her we shall. Tell me, Doctor, does it surprise you that a woman—even an insane woman—would be capable of inflicting such wounds as we saw today?"

Tina May seemed to be examining the tea leaves at the bottom of her cup. She did not reply for a few moments.

"I've long ceased to be surprised at what people will do to other people, Mr. Conigsby," she said.

Tina was halfway through her report when one of Detective Chief Superintendent Alec Conigsby's messengers came winging back with answers. This one, Detective Constable Tom Jones, was young, vociferous, and—on this occasion— loudly triumphant. "I've found her!" he said, bursting into his chief's holy of holies unannounced. *"I've nailed the girl!"*

"Tell," said Conigsby, deliberately unmoved and tamping down his half-lit pipe.

"Sir," said Jones, "County Police picked up a lorry driver near the junction of the M1 and the Coldshott Magna turn-off this morning."

"We had it on telex first thing," said Grant, who was also present in the office, having provided himself with a flimsy excuse to stay around. Noticing the way in which Tina looked up from her typing to eye the newcomer in an inter-ested and—so it seemed to him—appraising manner, he added gruffly, "He was mugged by a hitchhiker and suffered eye injuries. So what's new?"

"I checked in and saw him at the County Eye Hospital," said Jones. "Name of Jim Sutton. Fancied himself a bit of a stud, I should think—when he was in a better shape. Right now, he's in shock, which isn't surprising: he's blinded for life."

"Who did it?" asked Conigsby.

"A girl he picked up," answered the young detective.

"Description?"

"Not a lot, sir. Said she had green eyes. Staring green

eyes, he said. And that isn't all—he reckoned her eyes were insane!"

"How does that make her our girl for sure?" demanded Grant.

"I hoped you'd ask me that, Sergeant," retorted Jones. And he took from a paper carrier what looked like a bundle of light blue wool. "County Police had driven the truck to the pound, but hadn't got around to searching it by the time I arrived. I searched the cab and found—kicked away beneath a seat as might be in a struggle—*this* . . ."

Opened out and displayed to their view, "this" was revealed to be a woman's plain blue cardigan decorated with a single circle of dark blue diamond shapes.

"Well done, lad!" breathed Conigsby.

FOUR

At the end of her first day on the stall, the young woman who called herself Ruth had put in nearly twelve hours of hard and tiring work: in addition to washing up (and because of the shortage of storage space, mugs, plates, and the rest were required to make a quick turnround, so that this in itself was practically a full-time job during the rush periods), she also helped out at the counter when Norman was hard-pressed. This was not a part of the job that she greatly enjoyed, since it meant that she was under the constant scrutiny of the never-ending stream of customers.

In addition to the various items of food and drink, the stall also stocked a few lines of fancy goods: things like cheap dolls, windscreen stickers, cycle tyre repair kits, T-shirts, sunglasses.

She had a notion: "The sun's ever so strong," she remarked to Norman during a slack period. "I could do with some dark specs."

"Try these for size," he replied, and took down a pair from a display card. "There—they fit you a treat and you look like a film star trying to look like a nobody."

"I can't pay you now," she said.

"I'll stop it out of your first day's wages," he replied.

Norman was of the opinion that, come six o'clock and pub-opening time, the best of his trade was gone and it was flogging a dead horse to stay open after then. Accordingly, as the last of the customers drifted back to their cars just after six, he shut up the flap and called it a day. As Ruth did the last of the washing up, he cashed up the till and set aside a small pile of notes and loose change.

"Hold your hand out, Ruth," he said, and into her proffered palm he counted out one five and twelve one-pound notes, plus the change. "Twelve hours at one-fifty, that's eighteen pounds," he said. "Less forty-five pence for the stoppages—sunglasses—that makes seventeen fifty-five. Okay?"

"Oh, thanks," she said. And he grinned to see the delight in her face, if not in her hidden eyes behind the dark shades.

"I'm going to shut up and get off home now," he said. "Can I give you a lift anywhere? I mean, have you got any digs fixed up, and are you thinking of giving me a hand again tomorrow? I could do with your help," he added. "You're a good, clean little worker."

"I—I've nowhere to go," she admitted. "At least—not yet."

"It's too late in the day to start searching for digs," he said. "Look—why don't you doss down here in the stall? There's a couple of blankets and a cushion in the locker. You can bolt the door from the inside and no one's going to disturb you till I come knocking at half past five. What say?"

She nodded. "Yes, I'd like that," she said.

So it was done. When his old Austin 7 chugged off down the road, she was alone in the shut and shuttered stall. Alone, inviolable, and unseen. And with what to her was a small fortune tucked away in safety.

Apart from its nearness to Westhampton and all that meant in terms of peril, this was ideal, she told herself. Her only nagging worry was Norman. Would she have any—she jibbed at the very thought of the word—any *trouble* with him? She hoped not, for that could only lead to the thing she probably feared most of all—and there was plenty that she feared . . .

On her arrival back in London, Tina phoned Dr. Kettle, who asked her to come round. He lived in a two-floor maisonette converted out of a Victorian villa near Little Venice, with a view over the Grand Union Canal and the houseboats and narrow boats painted like fairground roundabouts. A professional cellist occupied the top floor; in the sultry spring evenings, the sound of his music drifted out through open windows. The housekeeper opened the door to Tina, and she found her teacher and mentor sitting hunched in front of the television set in his dressing gown. He looked round at her entrance, but did not get up. She thought that she had never seen him so wretchedly ill; in less than a week since they had last met, he appeared to have aged a decade.

He switched off the set and, giving her a tired smile, took her hand, drew her down, and kissed her cheek.

"How did it go at Westhampton?" he asked.

"Routine," she said. "But rather nasty." And she gave him a brief rundown on the double murder and its aftermath.

"I agree with your summation with reservations," he commented. "While conceding that a woman might, under certain circumstances, commit such a brutish crime, I stand convinced that no female, whatever her state of psychosis, would slay with quite so much fury for a handful of loose change. There has to be more to it, my dear Tina. It's possible that your lady with the green eyes committed mayhem upon the truck driver in defence of her honour. Did not a similiar situation obtain at—what was her name?—Mrs. Beverstock's place?"

"I wouldn't think it likely," said Tina dryly. "Not with the available characters: a crippled boy and a woman of late middle age, overweight and with an obvious cardiac condition."

"Perhaps you're right, perhaps you're right," said Kettle. "By the way, have you eaten? Mrs. Harker could rustle you up some cold beef and salad. Would you like to call her?"

"Thanks, I ate on the train, Johnny," she said, fondly reflecting how he was always solicitous about her well-being.

"Would you like a drink—a sherry? I had a dozen bottles from the TV company because they're so pleased with me. I only had to mention on the programme that it was my favourite tipple."

"No, thanks, Johnny."

"Did you hear the outcome of the Fawcett case, by the way?"

"No. Is it over, then?"

He nodded. "Thanks to your evidence, they nailed the blighter. Despite an impassioned plea from the defence (though what in heaven's name he found to be impassioned about, for the fellow's clearly a heartless scoundrel), Fawcett was found guilty and sentenced for life. He'll be out again in ten years, I shouldn't wonder, and knocking other gullible women off their perches for their savings."

"You look tired, Johnny," she said.

He conceded the point, which was so unlike his usual chipper self. "I'd have been in bed half an hour ago if you hadn't rung me, dear," he admitted.

"Come on, then," she said, taking his hand. "Up the wooden hill to Bedfordshire, and Nanny says you needn't bother to bath tonight, provided you say your prayers."

"I haven't said my prayers since I first fell from Grace," he said. "Though her name wasn't Grace. It was Mavis. Mavis Pullen. And the event took place behind the cricket pavilion at my old school."

"You're an old devil," she said fondly, "and also a shameless liar."

Together, they went up to his fine bedroom that occupied

most of the upper floor and was also his study and private laboratory. He eased himself into the great four-poster double bed and winced in so doing. She noticed with a slight pang of dismay that there was a clinical tray covered with a cloth on the bedside table. He followed the direction of her glance.

"Will you do the honours, Tina?" he asked. "A drop of the waters of Lethe to give an old feller a night's sleep without discomfort."

She nodded, removed the cloth, took up the hypodermic and the little bottle half filled with the clear liquid.

"How much?" she asked.

"Quarter grain."

She filled the syringe. So he was already walking the tightrope that spanned painless sleep and oblivion, having accepted that the question of morphine addiction was an irrelevance, for there was no longer any question of him going back.

"Why don't you marry me and succeed to my share of the estate, Tina?" he asked. "Or have I raised the issue before, and to no avail?"

"You've raised the issue before—and to no avail," she said. "Give me your arm, please."

She swabbed his arm and expressed air and a fine spray of the drug from the needle's end.

"It's a crying shame," he said, "that under the conditions of the entail, my share is going to revert to my bloody older brother when I drop off the hook. And to think that it could be yours." He clucked his tongue and pulled a funny mouth —a face-saver for them both: a pretence that he had made the proposition only half jestingly. But it didn't work for either of them, the small deceit.

"I don't want anything ever to be different between us, Johnny," she said.

"Because of that ex-husband of yours?" he asked quietly.

She shook her head. "What there is—what there ever has been—between Jock and me doesn't affect my feelings for you in any way, Johnny," she said. "And I'm greatly honoured by your offer. And very pleased."

He tapped the side of his nose clownishly. "By Jove, but the thought of all that bright gold must be demnably temptin', lass," he declared, after the manner of a Victorian melodrama heavy.

"La, sir," she responded in character, "but you do indeed know the way to the heart of a simple young country gel!

"And now, my dear," she said in her own voice, smoothing the sheets and his pillow, "it's time you relaxed and drifted off to sleep."

"Kiss me, Tina," he whispered.

She kissed him on both cheeks, and briefly on the lips.

"Good night, Johnny."

"Good night, Tina."

She cleaned the syringe and disinfected it, straightened up a few things around the room. By the time she had finished, he was already in a profound sleep. She picked up her hold-all and walked quietly to the door, where she gave a backward glance at the figure on the bed. His hands were folded across his breast like Caesar upon his bier while all Rome mourned him.

The very sight of police terrified her. They drove past the stall in their patrol cars, and she died inside at the thought that they might stop.

Thursday, as Norman explained to her, was early closing day in the nearby market town of Coldshott Magna, which meant that everything packed up around midday and the road past was like a wilderness. On that particular Thursday, he had half a mind to shut up shop and go to the pictures, indeed he had the thought to ask her—Ruth—if she'd like to come with him; but, somehow, though he

wanted to know her better, he had so far not been able to
break through her wall of reserve, so he dismissed the idea.
He took the opportunity of a quiet afternoon to drive over
and see his widowed mother and unmarried sister in Westhampton—leaving Ruth in charge. She watched him go
with mixed feelings: she felt safer on her own and free from
the risk of giving him an unwary answer to a casual question, but dreaded the prospect of being obliged to serve every customer who stopped by, and be subjected to their
close scrutiny—whoever they might be.

It was in this heightened sensibility of peril, with her every nerve stretched to snapping point and her fingertips doing a dance of death along the edge of the counter, that she
saw a police car turn off at the nearby junction and make to
pass by the stall.

In normal circumstances—if Norman had been with her
—this would have been her cue to duck behind the screen
that separated the kitchen sink from the counter and start in
on the washing up, leaving Norman to serve; no such solution was now possible to her.

She struggled for a few moments with the notion of pulling up the flap and declaring herself to be closed—but they
must surely have seen her by now, and the very act would
arouse their suspicions. She must stay put.

Both of them got out, said something to each other, and
sauntered across the road from where they had parked their
car on the opposite verge. Young fellows they were, both,
and one of them had hair so long that he was obliged to
have his peaked cap pulled right forward over his brow, so
that his back hair stuck out like a girl's chignon. She
touched her dark glasses to make sure they were firmly in
place and set to—quite unnecessarily—to cut some more
cheese and tomato sandwiches to add to the pile already on
display.

"Not very busy this afternoon, miss." It was the one with

the too-long hair who spoke. The other one was eyeing the space over the counter, as if he suspected that she was hiding someone there.

"Not very busy," he said again.

"It—it's market day," she faltered.

"That's right," he said. "That'd account for it. You must be a local. Live hereabouts, do you?"

"Yes," she whispered, dry-lipped.

"In Coldshott Magna?"

She nodded.

"Nice place, Coldshott. Where in Coldshott do you live?"

She, who had never been near the place in her life, sought out her quick options and found only one: "The—the market square," she said, her hands tightening round the handle of the bread knife that she was holding.

"Must be a bit rowdy on market days," he said, grinning. "You're best off here where it's quiet."

"Been working here long?" chipped in his companion.

"Yes," she lied. " 'Bout six months."

Silence. They both looked about them: at her, at the display on the counter. She tensed herself.

"What do you fancy, Alf?" asked Long-hair.

"I could do with a couple of cheese and tomato," replied the other. "And a nice cupper tea, miss, please."

"Make mine the same, love," said Long-hair. "Plenty of milk, but no sugar."

It was agony for her.

They had eaten their sandwiches, drunk their tea, and then asked for Eccles cakes and more tea, and all the time they lolled up against the counter's edge chatting away to each other, mostly about football, but occasionally touching upon their work—at which time the girl with hidden green eyes pricked up her ears to catch the slightest nuance that might relate to her. None came: they spoke of nothing and no one but "the Super"—a personage for whom they appeared to have mixed feelings and doubtful loyalties. And every so often, the better-looking of the two—the one with the decently cut hair—would break off and throw a remark or question at her, half flirtingly.

"Do they still have the Saturday-night hops in the Assembly Rooms at Coldshott, love?"

"Yes," she essayed.

"Do you go?"

"Sometimes." (That might be the safest answer.)

"Going this week?"

"I might."

"Might see you there."

"Mmmm."

The dalliance was cut short by a crackle of static from the open door of their car, followed by someone announcing a call sign. Long-hair doubled over to the vehicle and spoke into a microphone, following upon which he called over to his companion, "We're off!"

"Thanks for everything," said her would-be swain. "How much was all that?"

"One fifty-two," she said.

He took his change and grinned. "What number Market Place did you say?" he asked.

She panicked, said the first number that came into her head—and instantly forgot it.

He winked cheekily, and was gone.

Norman had promised to look in on her before she shut at six. He got back from Westhampton well before then, and was surprised to find the flap raised and the door closed on its mortise lock. Opening up, he found the interior in a pristine state, with all the food scraps disposed of in plastic bags, the washing up done, towels hung around to dry, the counter wiped clean.

But no Ruth.

An imp of suspicion made him think of checking the till. Before leaving, he had cleared it out, save for a "float" of a couple of pounds in loose change. With one hand on the drawer, he suffered a wayward feeling of unworthiness and left it alone.

They come and they go, he thought. And he just knew that she would not be back. On this account he felt oddly diminished.

Jock came home to Lochiel Street in the midafternoon and staggered straight up to bed, neglecting, for once—and blessedly—to call in on Tina and make a declaration of his continued and undying devotion—after particularizing, and in some detail, how her behaviour towards him had driven him to his present pass.

She was not sorry to receive a call from Jeremy Cook soon after, setting up again the dinner date which she had broken. He sounded grateful when she accepted for that very same evening (she would have supped with the devil himself—and Jeremy she did not regard as any devil, merely an enthusiastic puppy dog—rather than stay in to face Jock when he finally decided to show), and proposed they meet in the Goat and Compasses, a good pub off Chancery Lane much frequented by legal and journalistic people.

Tina shrugged herself into a silk paisley frock, wound a bandeau round her crisp curls, and ducked out of the house before her ex-husband, roused by the sounds of her toing and froing, came downstairs to investigate.

She took a taxi in the rain to Chancery Lane, arrived at the pub five minutes after the appointed hour, looked around for Cook, and found herself greeted by Marcus Struthers, who rose at the sight of her.

"Oh, hello," she said.

"Jeremy couldn't make it," he said. "Something cropped

up, so he asked me to meet you, explain, and give his apologies."

"Well, that's very nice of you, Mr. Struthers," she said. "I hope it's nothing serious—with Jeremy, I mean."

"No, no, I'll tell you about it," he said. "Do sit down and join me in a drink. It's the least I can offer, particularly after the way you handed me the Fawcett case on a plate the other day."

"That was nothing," she said.

"It was far from that," he replied. "What'll you have?"

He fetched her a drink from the bar, and she had the opportunity to study him for the first time without wig and gown—a costume that always seemed to her to reduce the wearers to the semblance of a flock of penguins.

Struthers was tall—over six feet. His eyes appeared to be deep grey. His hair was neatly cut, and very dark, with deep blue highlights, going slightly grey over the ears. She put him around a hundred and ninety pounds, with clear eyes that told of a healthy liver. And he would never have a weight problem. She was speculating on the state of his digestive organs when he returned with her gin and tonic.

"Your very good health. And thanks again," he said.

"And yours," she responded. "About Jeremy—you were going to tell me . . ."

He nodded. "It happened in chambers," he said. "We were just saying good night when the clerk from the partnership upstairs came clattering down in a hurry. His principal, Hamish Lattern, who's supposed to be in court tomorrow at ten-thirty with an extremely complex fraud case, had just been rushed off to hospital with a strangulated hernia, and would we take the brief because all the other partners are tied up?"

"It's just like in the movies," she said. "So you accepted the case?"

"Yes, but with considerable trepidation. The manner in

which the brief is drawn up makes the proverbial dog's dinner look like supper at the Ritz. There's five hours' work on
it, at least, before I can get to my feet at the Old Bailey
tomorrow morning and sell it to a learned judge. Unfortunately, I'm stuck with an important dinner tonight, but Jeremy gallantly stepped into the breach and volunteered for
the job, so . . ."

He met her eye. "I say, I really put my big foot in it then,
didn't I?"

"You did—just a bit," she conceded. "I'm afraid the
court can only award the Queen's Counsel beta-minus for
tact."

"What I really meant was this," he said doggedly. "You
two young people had a lighthearted arrangement that,
though its further postponement will cause a certain
amount of disappointment (and a great deal of disappointment to Cook, I can assure you), it is something you can set
up again at your mutual pleasure. What I have going tonight is a once only—and it's my head on a chopper if I
don't turn up. Am I forgiven?"

She smiled. "Case dismissed." And when she saw him
steal a glance at his watch: "If you must be going, don't
worry on my account. I can finish my drink at leisure and
grab a cab."

"I've plenty of time," he said. "The next train doesn't
leave till seven-fifteen. Dinner's not till eight-thirty, and I
can rely upon my wife to do the honours till I arrive."

"You live quite a way out of London?"

"Twenty miles," he said. "And, in my further defence,
the dinner party tonight is for the Lord Lieutenant of the
county and several other bigwigs who are making noises like
they are willing to back my nomination for prospective Par-
liamentary candidate at the coming by-election."

"That sounds very impressive," she said. "So you're going in for politics, Mr. Struthers? I expect we shall see you

as Lord Chancellor or Lord Chief Justice of England before
you're through."

He shrugged. "The robes of either office would be very
much my cups of tea," he admitted. "I am ambitious, and
quite unashamed of it. What do you think of that, Dr.
May?" He held her eye with a touch of—what? she thought
—defiance?

"I can only applaud your ambition. The really difficult-
to-get jobs in our society have got to be fought for. For
women, no matter what they say, it's still extra difficult. But
it's getting better. Not much better, but a bit." She put
down her empty glass. "And now you've got me on my soap
box," she concluded.

"Let's have another drink," he said.

They spent another quarter of an hour discussing their
respective professions and exchanging anecdotes; indeed, so
immersed was Marcus Struthers in his companion's account
of the fresh case in Westhampton that he lost track of time
till they both rushed out into the rain and managed to secure a taxi.

"Drop me at the station and stay with it," he suggested.
And this they did.

Only one exchange took place between them during the
short journey down the Strand:

"Of course," said Struthers, "to be ambitious, one must
also be prepared to sacrifice a great deal. Perhaps a very
great deal."

"Yes," she said. "You are so right." And she felt unbidden tears prickling her eyes. Fortunately, they had dried
before the taxi drew to a halt under the lit-up station façade.
They said good night and she wished him well at his dinner
party.

"Lochiel Street, Chelsea, please," she told the cabby.
"Number eighteen."

The phone began to ring almost as soon as she got into the house, kicked off her shoes, and put a kettle on for a cup of instant coffee.

It was Jeremy.

"Hi!" he said. "I had it timed that you would have just about parted company with his nibs. Did he catch his train?"

"Well, I presume so," she replied. "I didn't watch the going of it. How's the work getting along?"

He groaned. "I would sooner have kept our date."

"It was gallant of you to stand down so that your Leader gets his chance to impress the Lord Lieutenant," she said.

"Did he tell you all about that?" Jeremy sounded dismissive, and she instantly sensed intrigue. "I'm afraid that seat in Parliament is really a figment of poor Marc's imagination —and also in the imagination of the bitch he's married to. Pardon my lack of gallantry. Gallant to a fault, I'm always willing to make an exception in the case of Lady Miriam."

"Lady Miriam being his wife, I take it?"

"Mmmm." He did not seem disposed to further revelations, but pressed her to name another date for dinner. Tina hedged a little, pointed out (with some truth) that she was carrying the burden of Johnny Kettle's practice while he was ill, and that she had acres of case notes to write up, with only the evenings in which to do them. She finally got off the hook by promising to ring him in the middle of the following week, and sent him back to his work.

Jock did not pester her that night. And maybe, she thought, he was off again on yet another bender.

She made herself a light supper, watched the TV news, and had herself an early night.

The way things turned out, she was to stand in need of all the sleep she could get.

At about six o'clock the following morning, arrivals for the early shift at Messrs. Parkes & Whyte, Ltd., motor accessory manufacturers, finding a Ford saloon car drawn up in a lonely corner of their parking lot with its side lights on, went over to see if they could douse the offending beams and save the owner's battery. To their horror—there were two of them—the men in question found the body of a male party, a total stranger to them, lying slumped under the steering wheel of the Ford with his head almost severed at the neck and with appalling gashes on the arms and hands. On the passenger's seat adjacent to the corpse lay a blooded clasp knife of the kind that sailors use. A piece of stout cord was attached to it, for the apparent purpose of slinging the thing round one's neck or waist.

The police were there within minutes of being summoned, and certain procedures were set in motion, contingent on which Dr. Tina May was roused from sleep by her phone ringing well before seven.

FIVE

They sent her a car from the Yard, and it whisked her at a fine pace through North London, with two motorcycle outriders leading them through red traffic lights, up one-way streets the wrong way, and well outside the speed limit in the most disturbing circumstances arising from the beginning of the morning rush hour. Tina felt like royalty, and was accorded just such deference from the wide-eyed folks thronging the pavements and lining up for buses; though not, it has to be said, from fellow knights of the road, who glared through their windscreens at the speeding police car and its satellites and mouthed soundless obscenities.

Presently, they came to signs indicating the beginning of the M1 Motorway, and soon after that, turned past an Underground station labelled Cricklewood. Two blocks further on, a high wire-mesh fence announced the entrance to a factory complex that bore the logo *Parkes & Whyte, Ltd., Motor Engineers.* There was immediate and unchallenged access to a large parking lot that fronted the works buildings, and half a hundred vehicles were stationed there. All had been crammed down into two thirds of the available space, leaving one corner vacant at the far end, which was sealed off by a line of red tape strung out on portable bollards. There were several police cars present, as well as a command car: a sizeable van bristling with radio and TV antennas. Police, both plainclothed and uniformed, were present in abundance.

And the centre of the cleared space and the cynosure of

all attention: a modest blue saloon car, round which a pair of constables were erecting a canvas screen of concealment.

"Dr. May? We were told to expect you." That meant they had been warned she was a woman. The speaker announced himself as Arkwright, Detective Chief Inspector. He was red-headed, bespectacled, earnest in manner, with the suspicion of a keen intelligence that he kept well hidden, like a sword in a velvet sheath.

The men had rigged the screen by then, which provided privacy from the masses of people who were pressing their faces to the wire-mesh fence on all sides, but not a lot from those who had gained access to the upper windows and flat roof of the factory building nearest. Tina went behind the screen, took off her coat, rolled up the sleeves of her jumper, and put on a sleeveless white coat and a pair of surgical gloves.

"Would you like a cup of coffee before you start, Doctor?" asked Arkwright. And looked surprised when she nodded.

She had always been taught by Johnny Kettle to size up the job before one dived in and started pushing things around. That—and ask questions of anyone who chanced to be around. Minutes later, sipping a mug of strong coffee and looking in at the humped, bloody form bowed beneath the steering wheel, she asked, "What have you done so far, Mr. Arkwright?"

"Fingerprinted the door outside and in, Doctor. Also the wheel, dashboard, glove compartment door, and so on. No prints to be found. The knife—what we take to be the murder weapon—is still lying where it was left. And our fingerprint man is of the opinion that the killer has wiped the handle clean—but it hasn't been touched. Not yet."

She drained her coffee gratefully, having sized up the task.

Here we go, she told herself.

The car door opened easily. She peered inside, reached forward, and avoiding contact with drying blood that almost entirely masked the head and neck of the body, laid a bare part of her right forearm against the dead cheek. It felt —strangely warm. With no opportunity, at this stage, for a rectal reading, she put her thermometer in the sagging mouth and found the temperature of the body to be 101 degrees Fahrenheit, which was about three degrees *above normal!* Her mind ran to the thought of asphyxia, to which the rise of body temperature following death is a pointer. Had the victim been asphyxiated by exhaust fumes from the engine and then slashed with the knife?

Her eyes then fell upon the controls of the car heater, which were set to "on" and "hot."

"The engine was still switched on, and the fan heater running, though the engine was stopped," said Arkwright over her shoulder, as if in answer to her thoughts. "We switched off."

That would account for the body temperature, of course. The driver had halted inside the park with his fan heater at full blast because it was a cold morning. He had stopped the engine, and then made the switch again, in order to keep the heat level going in the car. Sometime after that, he was killed. And the body slumped forward—almost on top of the heater duct.

"How do you read it, Doctor?" asked Arkwright. "For my money, he only intended stopping here long enough to drop off his passenger, but was killed with his own knife. The killer then beat it, leaving the side lights on and the heater running. That's how it was found. The victim isn't known here at the factory."

"No doubt you've identified him already through the car registration," said Tina.

"Name of Richard Thomas Strong," said the other. "Occupation: sales rep for a fancy goods firm. The car's registered in his own name and he lives alone. Unmarried. Comes from Westhampton. And his hobby's boating. That accounts for the knife." He nodded to the supposed murder weapon. "Naval pattern. Buy 'em at any ship's chandler's. Anything else you want to do, Doctor—or shall we cart the body away to the mortuary?"

"Yes, there's not a lot I can do here," said Tina. "I'd put the time of death somewhere round about five, but the effect of the heater rather complicates the issue. What time was it turned off?"

"As soon as our patrol car got here in answer to a 999 call," said Arkwright. "About a quarter past six."

Gingerly, she picked up the knife between finger and thumb. A few head hairs adhered to the sticky blood on the blade and there was a ball of bloody fluff wedged in the pivoted joint of knife and blade: this might have come off the collar of the tweed jacket that the victim wore.

"Have them take the body out, please, Mr. Arkwright," she requested. "I'll take another look when it's laid out on the ground, and then it can be shifted to the mortuary for a full autopsy."

As the men were gingerly lifting out the corpse, Arkwright said to her, "This is going to be a tough one and no mistake, Doctor."

"Why do you say that?" she asked.

He nodded up the road in the direction that she had come in the taxi. "There's the tube station. Strong's a Westhampton man, so it's a hundred to one that he came down from there on the M1. Picked up a hitchhiker somewhere along the way, like as not."

"The killer."

"Yes. And as soon as they came to the end of the motorway, the killer asked Strong to drop him off in this car park because it's handy for the tube station. That's *one* good reason. And I don't think we're going to find him working for

Parkes and Whyte. It's my belief the car was parked here for the primary purpose of quietly killing Strong, and that his murderer then walked over to the station and took a train to the other end of London. That's why I say it's going to be a tough case to crack. We've got nothing to go on so far. The guy could have been a complete stranger to his victim."

"There's motive," suggested Tina.

"Casual robbery, like as not. And that's not going to be any great help," replied Arkwright.

The men had laid the limp body face upwards on a stretcher and the rest were crowding round it. They reacted as even the most hardened layman reacts to violent and hideous death:

"Christ! What kind of guy could *do* a thing like that to anybody?"

"What a bloody mess!"

Tina elbowed her way to the front of the crowd and looked down. Instantly, she felt the short hairs at the nape of her neck stir and prickle.

"The killer's a madman, that's for sure," said Arkwright.

"Or—woman," murmured Tina.

"What was that you said, Doctor?"

"Oh—nothing," she replied. "Let's get this thing to the mortuary, shall we?"

The body was loaded into a hospital ambulance and driven away out of the car park, past the rubbernecking crowds that now lined the streets at both sides and required the attention of police reinforcements to hold them back and ensure the movement of traffic.

So was Richard Thomas Strong, still warm, borne from the spot to which he had gone a few brief hours earlier, and surely with no thought, then, of the short life span left to him. Next came Flying Squad cars, the command car, and the car bearing Tina May and Arkwright bringing up the

rear. The fast-moving cortege was waved on through a red
light at the next junction, and past a vast hoarding announcing that Rowberrys—"Britain's Leading High Street
Grocers and General Purveyors"—were opening, on Monday, North London's biggest hypermarket on this site, adding as a footnote that there were vacancies for both experienced and inexperienced staff—a message that was of no
interest to Tina May and the police. Not to mention the
mutilated corpse in the leading vehicle.

There was no doubt in her mind, none at all. Nor had there
been from the first sight of the mutilations wrought upon
the head and neck of the commercial traveller.

Naked and rent, the body of Richard Thomas Strong
yielded its secrets to her highly professional gaze, and she
reckoned them up: the knife slash to the abdomen which
had lacerated the liver beyond all hope of repair; the cuts to
the throat and neck before and behind; the insane attacks
upon the eyes . . .

She straightened up and laid down her scalpel.

"I've seen this killer's work before, Mr. Arkwright," she
said quietly.

"Yes?" he exclaimed, surprised.

"Only the day before yesterday," she said. "In Westhampton. There were two victims then. The wounds were in
every way similar to these." She pointed.

Arkwright snapped his finger and thumb. "That would be
the woman and the young lad!" he exclaimed. "Mr. Conigsby's case. The Yard had a telex about it." He frowned.
"But we were warned that the suspect was a woman. Green
eyes. Cardigan . . ." His voice tailed off on a note of doubt.

"It was a woman, all right," said Tina. "She attacked a
truck driver later that day and half tore out his eyes. And
she left the cardigan behind at the scene of the crime."

"I'll pass this on to the Yard," Arkwright said, and

turned to go. "You're sure you're right, Doctor?" he asked. "About the similarity, I mean?"

"When one's accustomed to using the knife, there's never any doubt about technique," she answered. "These slashes are quite unmistakable."

Arkwright nodded, and went out to the command car, which was now parked in the yard. He was back in five minutes. Tina had just opened up the body and was cutting away the vital organs for laboratory inspection. The detective averted his eyes from the sight.

"I've also been on to the cheapjack firm that Strong worked for," he said. "He was due down here today at their head office with his weekly take, which, because these people mostly deal with small traders, is almost all in cash. It would be in his briefcase." In answer to her unspoken question, he added, "There was no briefcase in the car, which has been wiped clean of fingerprints inside and out."

"You don't need fingerprints, Mr. Arkwright," said Tina May. "The killer left her signature all over this body!" She slid a severed kidney into a small plastic bag and sealed it up.

"Ar, them's good people to work fur, but they don't 'old with any funny business, like. No pilferin'. Any pilferin' an' you're out."

"So I've 'eard, so I've 'eard," the woman's companion, next in the queue, retorted. "Friend o' my niece, she was caught at Rowberrys in Chingford, an' all she did was eat a chockie bar off'n a shelf and she was sacked on the spot."

"Mind you, like I sez, them's good people to work fur," reiterated the first woman. "Oops! Sorry, duckie, did I tread on your foot?" The remark was addressed to a young woman standing behind her, who won herself a second glance if only because she was wearing dark glasses in overcast skies and slight rain.

Receiving no response, and tiring of her other companion, the older woman returned to the initiative. "You done this kind o' work before, duckie?" she asked.

"No," came the answer.

"What was your last job?"

No answer.

"Remember to bring your card?"

Her addressee was spared the necessity of answering or not answering by the opening of a door before which the straggling line of women was queued. A cheerful-looking young man in a grey overall coat with a battery of pens and pencils stuck in the breast pocket, to which was pinned a plastic tag bearing the name Mr. A. Wright, stood regarding them for a few moments with obvious amusement.

Presently, he announced: "Right, I only need about six strong young women to lift and carry heavy loads. And I mean heavy, so some of you older ladies needn't bother to apply. Sorry. Better luck next time, ladies."

The injunction thinned the line by at least three quarters, including the pair directly in front of the young woman in sunglasses. Indeed, she was the third to pass in through the door, and within minutes was next to be entering an inner door marked *Personnel Manageress*. On the way in, she passed close by the girl who had been called before her. The other was coming out.

"Lousy bitch!" snapped the girl. "Told 'er what she could do with 'er bloody job, I did!"

After this unpromising introduction came the sight of a woman of indeterminate years seated behind a desk opposite. She was thin, bespectacled, hair dyed bright red and frizzed out in an Afro. She was telephoning.

"What? If she's causing you any trouble, get rid of her! I don't care if we open on Monday morning with half a staff. I'm having no troublemakers here while I'm in charge. Sack

her on the spot—or you'll be out yourself! And now put me
on to Mr. Starling!"

A few moments passed. The woman tapped the desk top
with the end of her pencil. Her bared nerve ends, the vio-
lence pent up within her, were palpable. Presently, as she
still waited for a voice to manifest itself at the other end of
the wire, her myopic eyes became aware of the figure looming at the other side of her desk. The eyes behind the thick
lenses panned over the newcomer and appeared—grudg-
ingly—to approve of what they saw.

"Name?" she demanded.

"Shaw—Eunice Shaw."

"You call me Miss Harlow!"

"Yes, Miss Harlow."

"Then what's your name?"

"Eunice Shaw—Miss Harlow."

"Card!"

The card was handed over. Miss Harlow tossed it on top
of a pile contained in a desk tray.

"Report to Arthur Wright!" she snapped.

"Yes, Miss Harlow."

Before she reached the door, the young woman who
called herself Eunice Shaw heard the Personnel Manageress
make her connection: "That you, Starling? Now, see here,
I've been given the job of getting this store staffed by the
time we open doors at nine o'clock on Monday morning,
and I'm standing for no obstructionism, do you hear me? I
sent you ten men for the cold store, and you will take them
—and *like* them . . ."

The cheerful Mr. A. Wright was not quite so cheerful at
closer acquaintance, for the task of imposing a work discipline upon fifteen or twenty young women who were going
to do the rough donkey work of hefting cartons of tinned
fruit and vegetables from the high shelves in the storeroom,

and loading them onto trolleys for transportation into the food hall, called for a ruthless breed of overseer. The work force, anyhow, was casual, disinclined to effort unless being watched, and destined to be transitory. Experience had taught Wright that superficial jollity overlaying complete ruthlessness was the way to handle them.

"My name's Eunice Shaw, and Miss Harlow said I was to report to you." It was the girl in the dark glasses whom he had noticed when she came in. Not a bad bit of skirt, he thought. A cut above the usual in intelligence. The sort who could make a good worker.

"This is the tinned fruit and veg department," he said, pointing. "Our shelves go from there—to there. The girls from the food hall come in with the trolleys, see? . . ."

In two minutes flat, he gave her the basic rundown on the job, and then introduced her to a black girl named Norma Brown, who was in charge of two long shelves and the four girls—Eunice Shaw included—who serviced them.

"He ain't a bad sort," confided Norma Brown when Wright had left them. "Only, make sure he don't catch you idling when there's work to be done. And if you want a ciggie, go and have it in the ladies'. He'll try to grope you if he gets a chance, but the way you handle *that's* up to you." A week of loading up the shelves in preparation for the Monday opening had given Norma a fair insight into the workings of the system. "And watch your step with old Mother Harlow," she warned. "If ever a woman deserved to be put on a bacon slicer it's that cow. Say, where you living, Eunice?"

"I—I haven't found anywhere yet."

"Just got here? Say, it's lucky you met me, gel. My ma, she's got a room that's going for fifteen poun' a week and breakfast thrown in."

"That—that sounds about right," said Eunice Shaw doubtfully.

"Come home with me tonight," said her new friend. "It ain't committing you one way or 'nother, and rooms ain't easy to come by in these parts."

Eunice Shaw nodded—still doubtfully.

Tina phoned Johnny Kettle from the hospital. His housekeeper answered the phone, but Kettle cut in on the bedroom extension.

"Tina!"

"Johnny, how are you?"

"Much better. I hear—they rang me from the Yard—that you've had another case."

"Johnny—it's the same killer . . ." And she blurted out her findings. He listened through to the end without interrupting, and then he said, "Tina, I'd like you to send me copies of your notes, pictures and all. Yes, I'm still in bed, but a little exercising of the mind can only be of benefit in my condition. I am bored!"

"Of course, Johnny," she said. "Oh, and we've had the press round here already. And would you believe? They want me to appear on TV tonight in the *Roundabout* programme. It seems that Scotland Yard is quite keen to publicize the connection between the killings and the maiming. They've even cooked up a name: they call it 'The Case of the Green-Eyed Woman.' What do you think—about me going on TV?"

"Well, if it helps to catch her, I suppose it's justified."

"Yes, except that, so far as I'm concerned, I'm pretty certain that, the female pathologist angle aside, the only real reason I've been offered the job is on account of my connection with you."

"So what?"

"It hardly seems fair—cashing in on your reputation, Johnny."

"Embrace the concept with both hands and hold tight,

my dear. After all—I've been grooming you to take over my TV slot when I've gone next year."

"Johnny—don't say that. Don't even *think* it . . ."

A lump came in her throat. The irony of it: that she could face the dead without flinching, but was thrown all in a heap by the dying.

A bright idea at the new Rowberry hypermarket was to provide a substantial midday meal at a nominal cost to all staff, the money deducted from their weekly wages in arrears. This was being launched as an experiment to cut down afternoon absenteeism and lateness. TV was also provided in the canteen, and turned off at 2 P.M. sharp, so that the staff could return to their labours.

That day—her first and last at Rowberrys—Eunice Shaw ate her shepherd's pie, peas, and baked beans with Norma and the three other girls from the shelves. The others chatted about boyfriends, wages, the shortcomings of the Rowberrys system; Eunice Shaw contributed nothing.

The tyrannical Miss Harlow ate alone in her office. Medium-grilled sirloin steak for her. At two o'clock exactly, she drained her coffee cup and rang for Arthur Wright, who, being none too prompt, won himself a sharp glance from his superior.

"Wright, take a look at this," grated the latter, passing over to him an employment card—the same one that Eunice Shaw had given to her that morning. "Tell me what you think of it."

Wright frowned and did as he was bidden. Almost at once, his slightly uneasy expression gave way to one of interest bordering on excitement. He held the card up to the light, squinted at it closely, rubbed at a piece of the printing with a fingernail.

"It's a bloody forgery," he declared at length.

"And a clumsy one at that," she said. "And mind your language!"

"Worst I've ever come across. And I've seen a few," he said, adding ingratiatingly, "And so must you have, Miss Harlow."

"I wonder how much she paid for it," mused the woman. "She must be pretty green. First time out of prison, I expect. Well, she hasn't got far at Rowberrys, thank God. I'll have her out right away with a flea in her ear."

"Going to inform on her to the fuzz, Miss Harlow?" he asked.

"No—don't want any trouble," she said. "Let somebody else sort her out. Just you send her in to me, Wright, and I'll get rid of her my way—and she won't forget it in a while."

Wright rubbed his chin. "If I can make a suggestion, Miss Harlow . . ."

"Yes. What?" The suspicious, defensive eyes glittered sidelong at him through the pebble lenses.

"Well, for all that, she's useful to me this afternoon," said he. "Why not let her keep working till quitting time and get the benefit of her? After all, Miss H."—he sniggered—"we won't be paying her, will we?"

She matched his grin with a tight-lipped smile of mean malice. "Yes, you do that, Wright," she said. "Let the slut work for us for nothing for the rest of the afternoon, then send her in to me. Any more job applicants outside? If there are, send 'em in. What with the Shaw woman, and three fellers that Starling's insisted on throwing out of the cold store, I'm going to be lucky to make up my numbers for Monday morning."

"You'll do it, Miss Harlow," said Wright, leering. "And I don't know anyone but you who could. You work wonders, you really do."

She smiled back at him, and patted her red frizz.

At six o'clock, Tina May switched on the radio news and was greeted by the announcement that police authorities nationwide had been alerted against the so-called Green-Eyed Woman, and that there would be a simultaneous radio and TV discussion at eight that evening on the implications of the case, at which officers from Scotland Yard and from the Westhampton police would be exchanging views with Dr. Tina May, the distinguished young pathologist, whose brilliant forensic detective work had revealed the truth that there was a triple killer on the loose.

Tina switched off the radio and readdressed herself to the problem of what she was going to wear on TV that night. She had had a bit of assistance from the eager young woman who rang her earlier with news of where and when to rendezvous. White was out. Too much jewellery was not a good idea. Be careful about too much décolletage. Leave the makeup to the studio. It all sounded simple enough. The choice clearly lay between—she slid open her fitted wardrobe cupboard—the silk paisley, and a wool jumper and skirt. If anything, she preferred the latter.

There came a tap on the door, which was bolted. She always bolted her door—and the good reason was standing right out there in the passage.

"Tina—it's Jock."

"Yes, Jock. What is it?" The older sister or brisk schoolma'am was definitely in order.

"May I speak to you for a moment, please?"

"By all means."

"May I come in?"

"I'm changing to go out. I can hear you quite adequately from where you are."

There was a pause. That would mean he was pulling one of his faces: it would be either the mad dog face or the Early Christian martyr face. Both were interchangeable in the circumstances.

"Tina, what I have to tell you is rather difficult." (It was mostly "rather difficult," particularly if the monologue concerned money. For a man who had once thrown bread rolls at a civic banquet hosted by the Lord Mayor of London, Jock could be very delicate in his approach when it came to sponging.)

She tried a single string of pearls up against the tan jumper, but the effect was too "county." The drop crystal pendant on the silver chain was better.

"You're not listening to me, Tina."

"Oh, yes, I am, Jock," she replied. "Do please go on. What's the proposition?" (She nearly added: "this time," but refrained out of a sense of delicacy.)

"How did you know it was a proposition?"

"I'm the seventh child of a seventh child and a bit psychic," she murmured.

"What's that you said?"

"Nothing."

"Well—it's like this. I met this Yank who was at school with my cousin Freddie . . ."

She could have set the sales pitch to music. Nothing had changed from the original format, only the characters and the bait. For Freddie who was at school with this Yank, read a guy who was in the RAF with old Pootles Malloy (you remember old Pootles, darling!) or a feller who played golf with Sniffy Warburton-ffinch—that whole dreary little army of good, reliable chaps and their impeccable connections. Her first introduction to the syndrome had been on their honeymoon: then it had been a super bloke who played Rugby for the Old Carthusians, and whose enterprise was directed towards a scheme for building an atomic power plant in the Arctic in order to control the weather in the Northern Hemisphere. The enterprise got no further than extremely well-produced prospectuses paid for by Jock

Hardacre, who also invested £200 in the venture and lost the lot. Nor did he ever replace Tina's engagement ring.

By the time she had done a bit of spit and polish on her shoes and slipped them on, the bait proffered by the Yank who was at school with cousin Freddie was revealed to be an undertaking after Jock's own heart—for it was no less an idea than to clone the masterpieces of the world's painting and sculpture by means of laser beams. Though incredibly expensive to produce, explained the great entrepreneur at the far side of the door, it would not be beyond the bounds of possibility—given some financial assistance from UNESCO and others—for a small-time public art gallery in, say, Scunthorpe or Pine Bluff to own and display Rembrandt's *Night Watch,* Leonardo's *Mona Lisa,* and Michelangelo's *David,* which would be identical with the original models.

Receiving no response to the notion, and maintaining a sulky silence for five minutes or so, Jock then lowered his sights somewhat: "Well," he said, "if you don't care to come in on the ground floor with this tremendous scheme, I wonder if you'd please lend me a fiver or a tenner to tide me over till next week?"

"Of course," replied Tina, forbearing to ask him what had become of the hundred and fifty that he had received the other day. "I'll leave it on my dressing table when I go out."

He grunted something and shuffled off, back up the stairs to the two attic rooms where she supposed he lived in unspeakable squalor, surrounded by unfinished novels and short stories whose great promises were fated never to be realized.

She waited till she heard his door slam, then, dropping a five-pound note on the dressing table, darted swiftly out of the house and hailed a taxi that came cruising down the King's Road towards her.

Doreen Harlow waited till it was past seven and getting dusk, till the last of the cleaners had gone and the three staff entrances had been shut and double-checked by the night watchman, who then tapped on her door but did not dare to open it.

"What time you goin', miss?" he called. "Just wannid ter know, like."

"About eight," she answered. "I'll let myself out. And do me a favour, will you? Don't wander around the place whistling and don't have that radio of yours blaring away till I've gone. I've got work to do. Do you hear me?"

"Yes'm." The old fellow sketched the ghost of a military salute at the closed door and hobbled away, fearful of placing his job in hazard with the gorgon of Rowberrys.

Alone again, she unlocked a drawer of her desk and, bringing out a quarter bottle of scotch, poured herself a brimming measure in an empty teacup, which she afterwards sipped at deeply and with considerable elegance, little finger raised at the handle of the cup as she perused with satisfaction the results of her day's labours.

Not bad, not bad at all. They would be pleased at head office. Good old Doreen, they would say. The stormy petrel of Personnel has done it again. Say what you like about Doreen: she's ruthless in her methods, but she gets her way in the end.

Yes, it had to be a record. Coming at the tail end of a strike, with most of the Rowberrys work force affected, she had been lumbered with the task of staffing a new and oversized shopping unit from scratch, with mostly inexperienced and casual labour stiffened only by a cadre of such people as Wright, Starling, and the rest . . .

The thought of Arthur Wright (he'd have to go: too familiar, and loose with his language) put her in mind of something that she could not quite recall. A piece of unresolved business concerning one of the staff. Tch! Her memory must be going, and not to be surprised at, what with all the responsibility that was thrust upon her.

She poured herself another cup of whisky and sipped at it luxuriantly, then paused with the cup still at her lips.

Someone was coming down the passage outside her door.

And it was not the night watchman, whose gait—informed by an old war wound—was quite unmistakable. No, this sounded more like the footfalls of a woman. A woman on—it was ridiculous at this hour, but—*tiptoe?*

"Who's there?" she called out.

The sounds ceased. Miss Harlow opened her drawer, placed the empty cup, saucer, and nearly empty bottle into it, and turned the key in the lock.

From where she was sitting, her myopic gaze could not register that the handle of her door was slowly being turned from the outside; no warning reached her till the door crept slowly open with a barely perceptible creak.

Miss Harlow was on her feet.

"Who is it?" she cried.

The door swung completely open, revealing the figure that stood there.

"Oh, it's *you!*" said the Personnel Manageress. "What are you doing here? Get out! Get out of my office at once!"

And then she began to scream. But not for very long— only till she choked on the blood from her ripped-open throat.

SIX

"I'm home, Mum!"

Home for Norma Brown was 13 Aladdin's Road, Neasden, scarcely five minutes' walk from the new Rowberrys hypermarket. Aladdin's Road had grown into a trim little outpost of the West Indies, with a heavy proportion of small-islanders. The Browns were from Barbados. Their magenta front door and pale lilac brickwork with its pointing picked out in white was a statement of individuality echoed by the equally strident colour schemes of their neighbours.

Norma embraced her mother in the narrow, neat kitchenette.

"Smells lovely, Mum. What is it?" On Thursday nights, it was always the same, but she liked to hear it said.

"Boiled leg of pork," responded her mother, enjoying the sounds also. "With black-eyed peas and yams. Green bananas and biscuit. How's that?"

"Mmmmm."

"You been to the Social Club? And take your fingers out of that saucepan, gal!"

"Yes, and I nearly had a white lodger for the spare room tonight, Mum. I was going to take her along to the club too, but she wasn't around at quittin' time. She'd walked out on me."

"Did you have a promise that she'd take the room?" asked Mrs. Brown.

"We-e-e-l—yes, I s'pose so. Leastways, she said it

sounded okay at fifteen poun' bed and breakfast, and she had plenty of time to back out during the day."

"Mebbe you pushed too hard, Norma, so's she couldn't say no without giving offence. And anyhow, maybe she's racial."

"Mmmm, I wouldn't have thought she was racial," said Norma. "But she is kinda—well—funny."

"What way's she funny, gal?"

Norma rubbed her cheek. "Well, she wears dark shades indoors for a start. Also—also, she has a way of looking away and not joining in when other folks are talking together—like she did when we sat and ate with Madge and the rest today. Yeah, I think she's—funny."

Mrs. Brown looked at the clock and wiped her hands on her apron. "Lay up the table, gal," she said. "Your pa'll be home anytime now, and there's a programme on the telly about that murder up at Parkes and Whyte today. We want to watch that."

"Everybody was talking about it," said Norma, opening the cutlery drawer. "It's real creepy, having a real-live killin' right on your doorstep!"

The director fussed around them after they had been made up. He was a would-be high-flyer named Gerald Hackett-Bryce and the idea was all his: to slot an immediate murder case into a weekly topic magazine programme; furthermore, as a protegé of Simon Elles, mastermind of Johnny Kettle's programme, he had a special interest in "bringing along" the highly intelligent, articulate, and attractive Dr. Tina May. They said—it was fairly common knowledge around the place—that old Kettle's health was failing and that he could well be considering retirement. There might be a case —and Simon held this view, had said as much over supper the previous evening in the St. John's Wood apartment they shared—for putting Kettle out to grass almost immediately and bringing the May woman into the programme. If a crusty old guy like Johnny Kettle could break through the shibboleths surrounding a subject like forensic medicine, what heights of popular entertainment and instruction might Tina May not scale with her blood-curdling tales and bits of long-defunct corpses?

"I think," said Hackett-Bryce, "that Toby introduces the subject, as per script. Then we have Mr. Conigsby sketch out the basic components of the Westhampton murders, citing Dr. May's conclusions. All you'll need to do at this juncture, darling"—addressing Tina—"is to look wise and nod a little. All right?"

Tina sat next to the star interviewer Toby Jakeman, who had imposed his stamp of Aggressive Enquirer after Truth on the *Weekly Roundabout* programme. Conigsby of the Westhampton police and Arkwright of the Yard flanked them to form a crescent shape before the main camera.

Glancing sidelong, she caught Alec Conigsby's eye, and he gave her a heartening, conspiratorial wink.

She had come far that evening, moving as quickly across London as the Underground railway would carry her, and nearly as far; doubling back along her tracks, switching from line to line till she emerged in a place she had never heard of called Peckham Rye, where she was obliged to pay to the ticket collector at the barrier a considerable amount of excess fare.

It was dark when she got out of the station, the sky black, moonless, and overcast above the eyeless rooftops of the shut-up shops; ever-open cafes, amusement arcades, sex shops, laundromats. A jukebox played reggae. A motor bus flashed past, sweeping the rainwater from the gutter and splashing her skirt. She saw the steamed-up window of a cafe across the street and went inside.

"What'll it be then, love?" asked the dwarfish man behind the counter, speculatively eyeing the girl with the dark glasses and the nervous air.

She asked for tea and—seeing them piled high on the counter, oozing their greasy fat like stalactites down the stepping-stones of thickly cut bread—a slice of bread and dripping, both of which she paid for and took to a seat in a corner at the far end of the room from a TV set, whose flickering image of an old Western movie was enthralling the establishment's clientele, numbering about a dozen.

Her tea was scalding hot. She blew on it and set the mug down again to cool. The end credits were flashed on the TV screen over a shot of the hero waving his hat in farewell to the heroine. She was tentatively nibbling at the edges of her bread and dripping when the titling and the tricksy introductory music of *Weekly Roundabout* came up and they panned in to a close-up of Toby Jakeman. She did not register a word he said—not till the name Westhampton slipped through the carapace of her self-absorption and she looked, wide-eyed, at a shot of a mean shopfront in a grimy terraced street, next at the close-up of a crudely lettered sign that hung over the premises:

E. BEVERSTOCK—*Fancy Goods*
Wholesale & for Export

And then the droning, self-confident voice caught up with her, and she was listening and watching like the rest of them in the cafe, all unaware and uncaring of the slice of bread and dripping that had fallen from her fingers, to land, dripping side downwards, on the dusty floor.

"She's pretty, darling. Your little lady corpse doctor's really very pretty. And you never told me, you old slyboots, you!"

Lady Miriam Struthers, daughter of an earl, society beauty and debutante of her year, wife of the tremendously up-and-coming Marcus Struthers, Q.C., and (by common consent of most of her so-called friends and all her acquaintances) a cut-glass, copper-bottomed bitch, was reclining in an armchair in her country house drawing room in front of the TV, a bloody mary in one slender hand and a pitcher of the same on a glass-topped table nearby for refills. She was, as always, dressed straight out of the current issues of the top magazines, in a subtle variant of a jungle guerrilla's combat jacket and pants, tailored in dyed silk and trimmed with real leopard skin at throat, wrists, and ankles. Pinned upon her expensively cantilevered bosom was the badge of her father's regiment of Foot Guards fashioned in white gold and the whole spectrum of precious stones.

Struthers sat opposite her. He had not changed, but still wore his formal city rig with the striped pants. He twirled a whisky glass in his thick fingers and gazed impassively at the image on the television screen.

"Quite charming," purred his wife. "So girlish and modest in her simple chain-store jumper and dingle-dangle. No wonder you fell over yourself to pinch Jeremy's date with her, sweetie. I shall have to watch you."

Struthers made no reply. Lady Miriam swallowed off her bloody mary, hiccuped, and gave herself a refill, eyeing all the while the ash blonde with the classical profile that filled the screen.

Off camera, Toby Jakeman said, "Tina—if I may call you Tina, Dr. May—do you think that the murderer—or murderess, as it seems we must come to regard the killer—is likely to strike again?"

"I don't know," replied Tina May. "It's an opinion that isn't within the scope of my discipline. A psychiatrist might answer your question with some conviction. I'm afraid I can't."

"Isn't she a perfect little bully?" said Lady Miriam, laughing. "Did she bully you, also, in court, Marc?"

"But if the killer strikes again, Tina," persisted Jakeman,

"you would be able to relate—how to put it?—her *bestial handiwork* to the slayings that went before?"

"Yes."

"Provided she—the killer—employed the same technique, of course."

"If the killer used a knife," said Tina May, "no matter with what technique, that which you describe as the 'bestial handiwork' would be quite apparent to the practised eye. As I have said before, it is the killer's signature and as ineradicable as the nuances of one's handwriting."

"Squish-squash again!" cried Lady Miriam. "Old bossyboots Jakeman has never been so talked down to on the box in all his career. I quite warm to your little girlfriend, Marc darling. We must have her round for drinks one evening. I don't think I could countenance her throughout an entire dinner party (though I've no doubt it would give you great delight), but it would be quite amusing to dent that outrageous self-esteem over a few snorts of gin. What do you think, sweetie?" Her green-eyed gaze panned over him mistily, eyelids drooping.

"I think you talk a lot of rot sometimes, Mirrie," he said without heat. "And you're drunk again."

"You bastard!" said Lady Miriam. "Drunk or sober, I'm your only chance in hell of getting to the House of Lords, and don't you forget it!"

"You're dribbling," he murmured. "All over your chin."

The Strutherses were—in the phrase of their friends and acquaintances—"at it again."

Meanwhile, by them disregarded, the innocent cause of the row continued to charm and impress the mass TV public.

The cellist was practising upstairs, but he did not disturb Kettle's concentration: the pathologist merely shifted his armchair nearer to the TV set and, so as to give to the

roundabouts what he had taken from the swings, turned
down the sound by a fraction for the cellist's sake. Live and
let live.

The detective fellow from Scotland Yard was holding the
floor at the moment, and Tina was listening with the absorbed attention that he knew so well: chin resting in her
hand, the fingers of the other hand toying with something—
in this case the edge of the chair arm—but not nervously,
more as an adjunct to deeper concentration, like a mantra.
God, how he loved that girl: dearer than anyone of his own
family; dearer, certainly, than his own life, which was being
measured out in quarter grains from that hypodermic over
there.

The Arkwright fellow was a bit pompous, a mite pushy.
This may have been on account of the other copper, who,
though not of that Praetorian Guard, the Yard, was nevertheless his senior by rank. He was also showing off in front
of Tina—that much was obvious from the way he constantly addressed his remarks in her direction:

"The Yard will be in constant touch with Dr. May in this
case and will call upon her services immediately should the
unhappy event arise of another killing or killings. Does that
answer your question, Mr. Jakeman?"

"Yep," nodded the interviewer. "But tell me now, Mr.
Arkwright, what special measures are you taking to secure
the early arrest of the killer?"

"I don't think you can ask him that," said Conigsby. And
when Jakeman threw him a look of outrage, the Westhampton detective added, "Sufficient to say that Scotland Yard,
the Metropolitan, London City, and Provincial forces are
united in a nationwide campaign to apprehend this killer at
an early date, and certainly before she—we are accepting
that it must be a woman—can greatly add to her list of
outrages."

"A moment, Chief Superintendent," interposed Jakeman.

"Are you implying the acceptance of a situation where there may indeed be further killings?"

"It would be a folly to pretend that this couldn't happen," retorted the other stolidly, and added, "And it's a possibility that would be much increased if even the broad outlines of our contingency plans were signalled on television."

The listening pathologist chuckled. "And ho-hum to you, Mr. Jakeman," he said. "Between one or the other of 'em, they're giving you a fair bit of stick."

The interviewer covered his confusion with a spot of bluster: "Let it not be thought—er—Chief Superintendent, that my colleagues and I regard this programme as common entertainment, but as enlightenment, and . . ."

"I'm glad to hear it, sir," replied Conigsby. "For we here tonight are not in the entertainment business. Neither Dr. May nor Detective Chief Inspector Arkwright and I . . ."

It all seemed set fair for quite a row—which is good TV and good entertainment, thought Kettle. And he decided that he would stay up and see it through. But, meanwhile, a drop of the waters of Lethe was called for . . .

He reached out for the tray containing the hypodermic and the rest, and was pleased to note that Tina was speaking again.

"She's lovely—*reely* lovely. Isn't she, Mum?"

The Browns were at table and eating their supper "afters," which was tinned peaches and condensed milk, with tea. All eyes were upon the TV and Tina May's profile.

"I saw her this morning," said Mr. Brown. "Watched from outside Parkes and Whyte's car park. Saw her as plain as I see you. Lovely lady, like you said, Norma. Working behind a screen, she was, but I saw her come out in a white coat like a dentist. Then they brought the body out."

"Did you see it, Pa?" cried Malcolm, the younger of

Norma's two small brothers. "The dead body, Pa—was it scary?"

"All blood an' all?" echoed his sibling Chris.

Brown *père* shook his head. "It wuz all covered up on a stretcher," he said. "Then along comes this lady doctor, this Dr. May. And she walks past me as close as I am to you. Yessir, a real lovely lady."

"If everybody would shut up," said Mrs. Brown, with commendable patience, "we could hear what she wuz saying."

Tina, with only a little prompting from Jakeman, had steered the discussion away from the inflammable topic of what measures the police were marshalling against the killer to that of the killer's modus operandi, a line which the mammoth viewing audience, conditioned by Tina's mentor in his sensational programmes, both appreciated and enjoyed.

"I followed the usual procedures," she said, "to determine if the victims in all cases were rendered unconscious by any means before they suffered the fatal woundings. I don't think I'm giving anything away when I say that Chief Superintendent Conigsby this evening handed me the report from Westhampton forensic laboratory. As one had anticipated, they found nothing. Mrs. Beverstock and young Harry Finch died by the knife alone."

A concerted intake of breath followed by gasps of horror greeted her words. Toby Jakeman, a professional to his fingertips despite the occasional tendency to overassertiveness, let the moment go by, hanging in the air like the scent of acid drops, before he moved in:

"What kind of a woman, one asks oneself," he said, with the air of somebody trailing his cloak, "could perpetrate such a crime in cold blood, and with her own hands?"

Conigsby was dead on cue. Producing from the briefcase

lying by his chair a large-sized envelope, he opened it up
and disclosed a sheet of card with a head drawn upon it.

"This," he declared, "is the woman in question, as seen
by Mr. Thomas Arlington, proprietor of the shop in Westhampton which the murderess stood outside long enough to
take down the address of Mrs. Beverstock's workshop. And
also as seen by Mr. Jim Sutton, a truck driver who gave the
woman a lift on the afternoon of the day in question—an act
of kindness which she repaid by blinding him during a fit of
manic fury. The likeness was drawn by a police artist attached to my division—to the directions of Arlington and
Sutton."

The camera zoomed in on the drawing, which was rendered in coloured chalks. It showed a woman of about
twenty-five, with mouse-coloured hair parted at the right-
hand side and brushed simply to just below the ears. It was
a serene face, some might almost have said a "good" face,
with fine bones, a straight nose, mouth perhaps a little too
wary. But it was the eyes that claimed attention and, mindful of the nickname by which the case was by then generally
known, the camera next homed in on the eyes alone, close.
They were widely set under well-shaped eyebrows. And
were of a clear, limpid green.

"That's her! That's her!"

The rest of the Brown family turned to stare at Norma,
who had leapt to her feet and was pointing at the TV screen.

"Norma, what you saying, gal?"

"What's this, eh, Norma?"

"Who's her, then?"

The girl gestured frantically to the portrait displayed
there, shook her head, made vehement gestures with her
other hand, stabbing out each word: "That's the girl who
was taken on today! The girl I thought I had as a lodger,
'cept that she gave me the slip! . . . What's her name?

Jeeze, I've clean forgot it. . . . No! I got it—Eunice—Eunice Shaw. That's her!"

She pointed again as the camera drew back and presented the whole face of the girl with green eyes.

"Put on a pair of dark shades—*and you've got Eunice Shaw!*"

The cafe proprietor never saw the going of her. When *Weekly Roundabout* finished, he went over and switched to the wrestling. Next he shuffled round and picked up the dirty mugs and plates that lay close to hand. When he came to the table where the young woman in the dark glasses had sat, he was surprised and affronted to see that she had scarcely touched the mug of tea, and went so far as to draw the attention of those sitting nearby to the slice of bread and dripping that lay vandalized—dripping side down and trodden on—by the abandoned chair.

"There ain't no pleasin' some folks," observed the near-dwarf, wagging his overlarge head from side to side and clucking his tongue. "Tch, tch! 'Asser trouble wiv folks nowadays. Too much money, an' too easy come by."

She ran, pell-mell, anywhere to get away from the cafe and the TV screen that had bared her secret. She ran in the streaming rain, recklessly crossing intersections, not looking left or right; splashing through brimming gutters, heedless of the traffic, the shouted curses, the blare of car horns.

Presently, soaked through and panting, her hair plastered in rat's tails down her cheeks, she steadied herself against a park railing and looked out across a sward of tended grass and leafy dark trees set against the skyline.

A pathway ran diagonally across the park and towards the trees. Casting a swift glance over both shoulders to make sure she was not observed—and there was no one out in that deluge of rain—she moved quickly along the path and mounted the steepening slope that soon was lost in a dripping tangle of undergrowth and overhanging boughs.

She plunged into the near-darkness, driven on by the terror of her plight, grateful only that it was like fighting one's way into a wet, remote yet oddly protective sanctuary against the encroaching world whose presence—in the way of traffic noises, lights, the hurly-burly of urban civilization —was fast disappearing behind her and giving place to darkness and silence.

Presently, the slope eased to a plateau, and the trees opened out to a clearing of tangled grass and dock weed. Worn out and trembling, she sank to her knees on a bed of pine cones that were crisp and dry in their shelter of spreading branches. She leaned back against the bole of a tree and closed her eyes, shuddering.

"It's no use! There's no way out for me! No escape!" She had said this to herself over and over again during her flight from the cafe. But now, alone in the dark silence of the night, with the teeming rain just out of the reach of her hand and acting like a protective cloak, she felt strangely safe and cosseted.

Surely, she thought, nothing can touch me here. I'm all alone.

Silent as a ghost, something that she took to be a dog or a large cat moved swiftly into the centre of the clearing and raised its head as if sniffing the air. She almost immediately registered it in her mind as a dog, and was afraid—for where there are dogs there are usually humans, and she feared for betrayal, imagining herself when its barking brought its master, and what of her plight when a torch was shone in her face—and she with not so much as a stick or a stone with which to defend herself? So she held her breath and watched the silhouetted shape in the middle of the clearing, terrified that it might detect her presence.

She need not have feared. The thing in the clearing was as

much an alien to the world beyond the fringes of the concealing woodland as she. No dog—but a fox, or, more correctly, a vixen, whose mate was even then foraging in the trash bins of suburban Peckham. She, who had never in her life seen a fox, and, though city-reared, had no inkling that the arch-predator of the countryside was settling very happily in its new urban environment, was greatly relieved to see the "dog" dart away back into the shadows from which it had come.

Weary, she closed her eyes again. And, presently, slept.

It was the old night watchman who discovered the body of the slain Personnel Manageress. Seeing the light still shining behind the door of her office, he tapped three times and, receiving no answer, let himself in.

"Sorry, miss," he faltered. "Not meanin' to disturb you, like—but I thought . . ."

He thought that she had fallen asleep and might even be glad to be awoken, never supposing for one instant—even when he approached the desk and looked down at the humped figure slumped with face buried in a mess of bloodied papers—that she was eternally beyond the scope of his voice and hand, for he was too shortsighted to comprehend the jazzy pattern of blood and paper. Receiving no response to his third time of addressing her, he found the temerity to touch the still-warm shoulder, and when that did not summon her, gave the shoulder a quite vigorous shake, whereupon the late Miss Doreen Harlow slid sideways, showing her face briefly and bestowing upon him a rictus grin that nearly stopped his heart beating. The corpse then slipped to the floor with slow, monumental grace.

When he had sufficiently recovered as to be able to pick up and hold the phone, the old night watchman dialled for the police, who summoned Detective Chief Inspector Arkwright of the Yard, and incidentally Tina May, who, along with Detective Chief Superintendent Conigsby, was dining with Toby Jakeman at the Gay Hussar restaurant in Soho. The interviewer called out to the waiter to charge the meal to the TV company and raced after the others in order to be —as the phrase has it—"in at the death."

SEVEN

Tina woke shortly before noon. The overnight rain had stopped and it was stuffy in her bedroom, so she flung open the window and peered out across the unkempt garden that Jock was always going to landscape with statuary, fountains, and formal herbaceous borders outlined in box hedging. A kind of miniature Versailles. When he got around to it.

She slipped out of her nightdress and stepped into the shower, her second in less than twelve hours. The last one had been at the forensic laboratory, after the autopsy on the —what was her name?—the Harlow woman.

They had gone there straight from the restaurant, and the insufferable Jakeman had insisted on accompanying them, no doubt with the intention of braying about the experience at his very next appearance on TV. Jakeman, however, had had his comeuppance immediately upon entering the autopsy room. At the first sight of that naked and lacerated corpse laid out on the japanned porcelain table, the star interviewer had fainted clean away.

She soaped herself generously under the tepid spray, then turned on the heat. The Woman with the Green Eyes had struck again. There was no doubt. The signature of the wounds was as unmistakable as ever. Poor little Miss—um —Harlow. Nothing was known of her as yet, save that she was a longtime employee of the chain grocers who had opened a hypermarket only a few blocks away from Parkes & Whyte, scene of the previous killing. Oh, and the poor thing was totally hairless (the shock of red frizz being a wig) and a virgin. The slayer's fourth kill.

Tina dried herself and slipped into a towelling robe. On the way past the hall table, she picked up a couple of envelopes addressed to her. In the kitchen that she shared with Alice, she was delighted to see that her flatmate had, for once, done her own breakfast washing up. The gesture was heightened by a note propped up against a biscuit tin on the dresser:

> Ducks – Saw you on TV. You were simply *fabulous!* Felt so proud of you. The little bastards of Form 2B will treat me with a new respect today. Nothing like being a friend of the famous. It rubs off! Love, A.
>
> P.S. His nibs was clattering round upstairs last night till long after 3 A.M. Sounded as if he was packing up to move. (You should be so lucky!)

She made herself coffee and toast, deciding to skip luncheon. There were case notes to be written up, and she really must ring Johnny and give him the latest news. Sitting down at the kitchen table, she took a sip of the coffee and opened her mail. The first was a reminder from a learned society of which she was a member that her subscription was overdue. The second bore the letterhead of a firm of solicitors hitherto unknown to her: Samuel, Smiley, Todd, and Arundel.

> Dear Dr. May,
> We are acting for Dr. J. Wakeman Davis, L.R.C.P., whose first wife, Mrs. Teresa Anne Davis, died in January of last year. Cause of death, entered by her general practitioner, was stated to have been "cerebral thrombosis." Mrs. Davis, a lady of 64 years, left her considerable private fortune to her husband, a man some years younger than herself. Dr. J. W. Davis has since remarried, to his receptionist, the former Miss Alison Cooke.
>
> The family of the late Mrs. Davis have applied for, and been granted, leave for the exhumation of her body, which is interred in Sawyer's Green Cemetery, London, S.W. 8.

These are the facts of the matter. Dr. Clive Warburton-Fosse has been retained by the Home Office to carry out the exhumation. This firm, representing Dr. J. W. Davis, wishes to retain your good self to hold a "watching brief" at the exhumation, which is to take place at 6:00 A.M. (0600 hrs.) on Saturday, 12th instant.

We regret the short notice, which is due to circumstances beyond our control, and would be greatly obliged if you would telephone your acceptance (or otherwise) at your earliest convenience. Since, as we understand, you do not drive a car in London, the present writer will be pleased to pick you up at 5:30 A.M. and convey you to the cemetery.

> Yours faithfully,
> J. A. Barden (Mrs.)

She knew of Warburton-Fosse, if not at first hand. He and Johnny Kettle were contemporaries, and their careers had run a close parallel, save that the former acted almost exclusively as an expert witness for the Crown, while Kettle had always been a "free lance," in which capacity the two men —rivals—had crossed swords many times in court on matters of forensic dispute. She remembered Johnny's frequent remark that Warburton-Fosse was a man whose considerable talents had been overtaken by his overweening vanity and his almost paranoiac horror of being bested over a professional judgement. And old Clive, averred Kettle with a certain wry amusement, loathed his—Kettle's—guts. It was this fact that in itself prompted Tina to ring the solicitors right away and accept the "watching brief" for that very same night. She had scarcely replaced the receiver when Kettle was on the line.

"Johnny! You must be psychic. I was just going to call you. Actually, I've only just got up. Didn't get back here to bed till four."

"I heard all about it. They rang me from the lab. It was another one of your killings, yes?"

"Absolutely, Johnny. It was uncanny. Honestly—I've never seen such carbon-copy wounds. Whoever she is, when they find her, she'll be found to be insane, that's for sure. But—my dear, how are *you?*"

"I'm fine. Fine. Don't fuss, girl. Listen—what are you doing tonight?"

"I'm due at an exhumation at the crack of dawn tomorrow. Nothing to do with the big case."

"Where's it at—the dig?"

"Sawyer's Green."

"No problem. Come round and have dinner with me at eight. I'll send you back early for your beauty sleep."

"I'd love to."

"An old patient of mine slaughtered one of his prize Aberdeen Anguses the other week, and out of charity he's sent me a sirloin of prime Scotch beef. It's only a smallish piece (it would be, coming from that bloody skinflint!), but the two of us can make a feast off it."

"Can I come earlier and cook it, Johnny?"

"No, m'dear, Mrs. H. is doing the honours in that direction. You just turn up looking like a million, and in time for a preprandial drink while listening to me propounding a theory which is going to stand your Case of the Green-Eyed Woman on its ear."

"You don't say! Do tell, Johnny!"

"Tonight. You'll have to wait till tonight. I'm not going to be cheated out of the look in your big brown eyes when you hear my theory."

"Autocrat! And my eyes aren't brown, they're blue-grey."

"I know they are. I was just trying to catch you out, to make sure you're awake. No time for further chatter. Mrs. H. is by my side and importuning me to decide upon what vegetables we'll have with the beef tonight. Do you have any particular fancy, Tina?"

"No—I leave it to you."

"Then it's *au revoir* till eight. And don't be late."

That afternoon, she worked on her report of the Harlow autopsy. With some small differences, it was only a rehash of the previous ones, and she paused only to listen to the five o'clock radio news which gave a guarded outline of the most recent killing, together with the information that no less than four people who claimed to be able to identify the Woman with Green Eyes had come forward and were being questioned by Scotland Yard.

At five-thirty, all hell broke loose.

First came a ring on the street doorbell. Jock came bounding down, three steps at a time, to answer it, where-upon his huge voice bade the unknown visitors to "Come right in, chaps, and mind your dirty boots because the little woman's rather fussy," and "Follow me, the stuff's not very heavy." After that, surely no fewer than another four equally heavy-footed men pounded upstairs to the attic with him. Tina took the opportunity to pack up her papers and typewriter (she had been working on the kitchen table), darting across the passage into her own quarters and lock-ing the door. She then put her mind to what she would wear for dinner that night—a choice that was strained as much by the resources of her imagination as by the limits of her modest wardrobe. In the end, she plumped for a trouser suit in bottle-green velvet. During this time, the personages up-stairs carried on a continuous thumping and bumping, punctuated by shouted orders from Jock.

She had scarcely begun to dress when they started to come downstairs again. And again. Each time clearly carry-ing, two by two, most bulky weights, to a dialogue whose burden was: "Up a bit your end, Fred," and "Steady round the bend, Alf." The final descent was accompanied by Jock, who added his own stentorian instructions to the enterprise. When the street door closed, it closed upon his voice in mid-cry. And it did not open again.

Alice let herself in soon after. She had stayed late at school to correct essays.

Tina greeted the friend of her girlhood with: "Jock's left home. At least, I think he has. He's had all his furniture taken out, anyhow."

Alice smiled and laid down her briefcase. "What could be nicer?" she asked. "You're shut of him at last." Her pretty, guileless face clouded. "It couldn't be all that easy, could it?" she said. "You couldn't get rid of him just like that."

"I don't expect so," admitted Tina. She had been thinking along those lines since the door shut behind her ex-husband.

"Fancy a cup of tea?" asked Alice.

"I'd rather have a large gin and tonic somewhere away from here," said Tina.

"You talked me into it, you smooth-tongued Siren," said Alice. "Get your skates on and we'll go over to the Chelsea Tailor."

While Tina and Alice were talking old times and Jock over their gin and tonics in the discreet lounge bar of their local pub, Conigsby and Arkwright were still at work in Scotland Yard. That afternoon they had been closely questioning selected members of the public who, in answer to the appeals on TV and in the press—and particularly to Conigsby's dramatic production of the killer's likeness—had phoned in with claims to have encountered the Woman with Green Eyes. One still remained to be seen—he was travelling down from the Midlands in a police car—but three they had already interviewed, and it was these they were discussing over cans of beer and sandwiches in Arkwright's office, which they shared as a joint command post.

"Well, let's see what we have so far," said Conigsby, "and decide if it all adds up."

His companion breathed on his glasses and polished them

with his handkerchief. Having set them back upon his nose, he perused the papers before him.

"The girl Norma Brown," he said. "Now, her testimony of identity will hold up alongside her foreman Arthur Wright's, even though Wright claims not to see the resemblance between the so-called Eunice Shaw and the face in the drawing."

"There are the other girls in Brown's section," said Conigsby. "Some of them had lunch with our suspect. If Brown makes a positive identification at a parade, they'll corroborate it for sure. By the way," he added, "any news on the fingerprints?"

For answer, Arkwright stabbed a bell push, which brought an eager, shirt-sleeved young officer, who responded to a mere raising of the eyebrows:

"Harlow's office—no dice, sir," he said. "And the shelves in the storeroom are a mass of smudged prints. Our only hope is to find Eunice Shaw's dabs on a carton of fruit or veg that she moved yesterday. Trouble is, they've already been moved out to the food hall, the cartons emptied, and the tins stacked by other hands on what they call the vending shelves."

"What happened to the cartons?" This from Arkwright.

"Stacked in the yard outside, sir, ready to be taken away for recycling."

"How many of these cartons?" This from Arkwright.

"On a rough count—fifteen thousand, sir." The boy's voice carried a dying fall, a desperate note of appeal.

"Get to work, then, Arthur," said Arkwright. "Somewhere in that stack are quite a few cartons bearing Eunice Shaw's fingerprints. You might be lucky and pick one out first off. On the other hand . . ." He shrugged.

The boy Arthur departed with a commendably light step, and the two detectives returned to their deliberations.

"We have Walker," said Conigsby, "who just happened to

be passing the Rowberrys last night at about half past seven, quarter to eight, and saw a woman coming out of the staff doorway—the same one that night watchman Higgins found unbolted on the inside shortly before he discovered the body. What do you think?"

"Walker I don't fancy," replied the other. "Number one, the barman of the Lord Nelson pub testifies that the guy had obviously had a drop or two when he arrived there at eight o'clock, and was in such a state by ten that they refused him any more drink. Add to that, he has no fixed address, and I've got a copper's built-in aversion to guys who drift from one doss house to another. Furthermore, his description of the woman he claims to have seen isn't worth much. He was vague about her height, build, what she was wearing. And couldn't say for sure if she had on dark glasses or not. Right at the bottom of the pile goes Walker, say I."

"Agreed. Which brings us to Tranter. His testimony— also uncorroborated—that he was stopped by Eunice Shaw at about seven o'clock yesterday morning is quite promising, since it seems to tie in the two murders, time-wise and place-wise. Let's presume she had a lift down the M1 with Strong. Murdered him to cover her tracks. She sees any one of the hundred posters for the new hypermarket plastered round the district. She needs a job. So she asks the way there and applies. You don't like my scenario?"

"I like better that she takes a train and puts as much distance between her and the murdered Strong as possible," replied Arkwright after a while. Then, remembering the disparity between their ranks, he added, "With the greatest respect."

"You're right, at that," conceded Conigsby. "But remember—we are dealing with a nut case, and there's no accounting for nut cases in the matter of logic. That's what makes 'em so difficult to catch. I mean, let's face it—the last place you were looking for Strong's killer yesterday was a few blocks down the road at Rowberrys. So you could say that, with the crazy logic of the insane, she picked the safest hideout around."

"True," agreed Arkwright glumly, and took a deep draught of his beer.

"However," said Conigsby, "as you were able to point out after we'd interviewed him, Tranter is hardly the kind of guy you take home and introduce to Mother. What's his form again?" He turned over a sheet of typescript. "Grievous bodily harm—two years. And again in 1982, but was acquitted. Two charges of attempted rape. Indecent exposure . . ." He spread his hands.

"He could have made up the story of his meeting with the woman to ingratiate himself with the police," said Arkwright.

"A lot of 'em are at it—and Tranter has stool pigeon and grasser written all over him."

A contemplative silence followed.

"And then there's Norman Blakely," said Conigsby. "They think very highly of him as a character and a witness up in Westhampton. He identified her from the TV shot as the woman calling herself Ruth who worked on his stall for two whole days. He even provided her with the dark glasses from his stock. What he can't tell us about her in the way of identification won't be worth telling. *And* we've got the corroboration of the two police officers who chatted her up on the last afternoon that she cut and run and came down to London."

"Blakely should be here anytime now," said Arkwright, glancing across at the clock on the wall.

It was getting on for seven in the evening.

Two drinks and Alice got quite garrulous. Maudlin, too. But, then, she frequently did. And the poor darling, thought

Tina May, had had an unfortunate life: what with that disastrous father (cashiered from the Army, died in a Home for Alcoholics, and Alice's mother had had to take in lodgers to put her through their rather snobby little private school), the calamitous affair with a married man who walked away with the money she had raised from selling her flat, so that when it was all over Alice had been glad to share with her old school chum with a weird ex-husband up in the attic. Small wonder that she had turned for consolation to the lunatic fringes of Marxism.

"Poor old Tina," she said. "We're both alone now."

Ye gods! Did she honestly think that there was the vestige of anything left of her feelings for Jock? Discounting a certain compassion for a boy who had never really grown up, who had a modicum of writing talent—quite enough to provide him with a decent living, but not a hundredth part of enough to satisfy his love affair with fame and fortune, so that he, like Alice, had to look elsewhere for consolation. Which was, in his case, booze.

"I must go, Alice," she said. "Don't worry about me. I said goodbye to Jock at the courthouse door. What's happened since has just been a rerun of an old story with actors instead of people. No, I really must fly, or I'll be late for dinner with Johnny. 'Bye, love."

The air in the King's Road was like vanilla ice cream, with a tang of coolness after the rain. There wasn't a taxi in sight, so she walked as far as Sloane Square and picked one up off the rank. She was at Little Venice well before the appointed hour. And no sooner had she opened the gate than she knew that something was wrong. Maybe it was because the cellist wasn't playing.

Mrs. Harker answered the door. She had been crying.

"What's the matter?" asked Tina. And almost immediately she knew the answer.

Johnny had been taken ill quite suddenly, at about the

time that Alice and she had gone over to the Chelsea Tailor. He had been sufficiently in command to diagnose himself: a mild coronary. Also, he had instructed Mrs. Harker to phone for an ambulance.

"They took him away," wept the woman. "Last thing he said to me was: 'Don't forget to ring Dr. May,' he sez. 'Tell her we'll have to postpone dinner and have the beef cold with salad, but it won't be the same.' Always the one for a joke is Dr. Kettle." And there came a deluge of tears.

Tina rang through to the hospital and the news was good. Johnny was sleeping peacefully, which meant the attack was no more than a warning. To a man already condemned to death within a year, the warning might be regarded as an elegance, she thought.

It occurred to her to phone Johnny's only living relation: the older brother, who lived in York. She tried, but all the lines to the North were engaged. It was then she remembered that Johnny and the brother had not spoken for twenty years. And Mrs. Harker called her from the kitchen.

The woman was standing by the electric stove, the door of the oven open and a handsome joint of beef lying there in its tin of gently sizzling fat.

"It's done," she said. "Brown on the outside and rare on the inside. Just the way the doctor likes it." And she began to cry yet again.

Tina carefully prized off a small piece of loose meat and put it in her mouth. Instantly, her taste buds reacted to the succulent flavour and texture.

"Lay table for both of us, Mrs. H.," she said briskly. "We'll eat it together. Like he said, it won't be the same cold, and you know he hates waste more than anything in the world."

And then she, too, was crying.

At about the time that Tina and the housekeeper were tack-
ling the washing up, a woman in her early thirties entered a
South London police station and went up to the duty sergeant at the desk. A man of mature years and experience, he
ran a knowing eye over her and had her docketed right
away: working-class and house-proud, with a husband
drawing a big wage on overtime; three holidays a year, one
of them abroad; probably owns a caravan and a small boat,
or both. Smokes a lot and also drinks. Wouldn't say no to a
bit on the side—it shows from the way she dolls herself up.

"Yes, ma'am. Can I help you?"

She lit a cigarette with hands that wavered slightly. He
did not draw her attention to the "No Smoking" sign, but
continued to gaze at her with a relaxed, avuncular expression that brought out the best in clients of her age, sex, and
class.

"It—it's my little girl," she said at last. "I'm worried out
of my mind and I daren't tell my husband. You see—she
hasn't come home."

He sighed. With the kind of freedom available to kids
these days and with wives who went out to work, it was a
wonder that kids didn't stay out in the amusement arcades
and discos right round the clock. Missing kids was one of
the biggest—and generally least rewarding and most time-
wasting—items in the book.

He pulled the book towards him and moistened his pencil
between his lips. "Name, please," he said. "Yours first."

"Mrs. Underhill. Mrs. Gloria Underhill."

"Address?"

"Bolsover Street. Number eighteen."

"Would you believe it?" he said. "I was born in Bolsover
Street. Number twelve. Ain't it a small world?"

Her nervous, painted lips sketched a travesty of a smile.
She took another strong drag on her cigarette and whispered, "Yes."

"Child's name?"

"Darleen. Darleen Underhill."

"Age?"

"Eight."

He looked up sharply. Eight was a bit on the young side to go missing.

"When did you last see—er—Darleen?" he asked.

"Last night." She said it so quietly, and he was so unbelieving of what he *thought* he heard, that he made her repeat it: "Last night."

"Darleen went missing last night," he repeated. "What *time* last night?"

"She—she wasn't home from school when I got back from work at six," she said.

"So what did you do?"

"Well, when she wasn't back for her tea, I went out to look for her. In the places that she goes to, like. The park. The amusement arcade in the High Street. Then I knocked on the doors of some of the kids she's at school with. None of 'em had seen her."

"So—what did you do then, Mrs. Underhill?"

She did not reply at once, but clumsily stubbed out her cigarette in the ashtray that was provided for the express use of folks who came in smoking. She then lit another. The sergeant watched her keenly. It seemed to him that here was a woman who was jacking up her courage to tell a big, round lie.

"I—I got me husband's supper," she said.

"And you didn't tell him that Darleen wasn't in," he said. "What *did* you tell your husband, Mrs. Underhill?"

"I—I said she had the bellyache and I'd put her to bed," she whispered.

A long silence, and then: "Why did you tell him that?"

Her eyes flared. "I was scared!" she cried.

"Scared—of what?"

She lowered her gaze. "Of what he'd do to the kiddie—for stopping out."

"And—what he'd do to you, perhaps?" he asked quietly.

She nodded, head still bowed.

"Is he a violent chap, your husband?"

Another nod.

"Knock you about, does he?"

"Yes."

"And Darleen?"

"Yes."

"Why does he do that, Mrs. Underhill?"

"Because . . ."

"Yes?"

"Because she's not his kiddie. I—I had her before I married him, and . . ."

"And what, Mrs. Underhill? You were going to add something."

She met his eye. Hers were defiant. "I wasn't married when I had Darleen," she said. "And Gary—that's my husband—he holds it against me. And her."

A young constable came out from the rear office, picked up a form from a tray, nodded to the sergeant, cast an appraising eye at the woman, and went back the way he came.

When the door had shut on the intruder, the sergeant said, "Where's Gary now, Mrs. Underhill?"

"Out with his mates, playing pool," she replied, and there was a touch of contempt.

"And he still knows nothing about Darleen?"

She shook her head.

"He'll have to be told right away," he said. And when her eyes showed fear: "Don't worry, we'll tell him. You can stay here in the waiting room while a constable goes and fetches him. All right?"

She nodded. But her fear was by no means lessened.

Ninety percent of missing children cases are cleared up within an hour of being reported. For the remaining minority there is a special procedure which comes into the category of High Priority. The sergeant connected straight through to his Divisional H.Q., gave the name of his station, his own name, rank, and number. Then a brief rundown of the facts.

After that, the system moved swiftly and smoothly into action, leaving the sergeant with nothing to do but radio his own cars and foot patrols and instruct them to look out for Darleen Underhill, aged eight, slight build, brown hair, brown eyes, dressed in a green mackintosh. And to pick up the father at the Working Men's Club and bring him in.

The young constable from the rear office, who had just taken a cup of tea to the woman in the waiting room, said, "Sarge, if you don't need me right now, I'd like to take a walk up to the park and see if I can find anything. The wood up in the top end—know what I mean?"

The sergeant nodded grimly. They both knew what he meant.

EIGHT

She was drowning, fighting for air and rising up through the cold sea wrack with the sound of a bell buoy clattering in her ears that stayed with her till she was delivered onto the alien shore and left there, shivering with exposure.

She reached out and switched off the muted bleeper of her alarm clock. During the night, she had lost all her bedclothes in her tossing and turning. The central heating had not yet come on. It was five by the clock and the rain was drumming against the window in a manner that promised a cold, wet dawn in the graveyard. She swung her feet out of bed and padded to the kitchen to put on some water for coffee. Her next thought was to ring through to the hospital. Stressing that she was "Dr." May, she enquired of an unenthusiastic night nurse and elicited the information that Johnny had had a good night and was, in the formula phrase: "as well as can be expected."

It was spot on five-thirty when, dressed in a lined mackintosh, rain hat, and thick gum boots, with two cups of coffee and a couple of slices of hot buttered toast inside her, she answered the ring of the doorbell.

"Hello. Good morning. I'm Janet Barden. Not a very nice morning for it, I'm afraid." The solicitor was fortyish, plump, motherly. She wore a short leather car coat and headscarf. Her pink face was good-humoured, her eyes watchful and intelligent. She took Tina's work bag and laid it in the back of her red M.G. sports. Minutes later, they had crossed Battersea Bridge and were travelling south, tyres hissing on the wet, empty road.

"Saw you on the telly the other night," said Mrs. Barden. "I don't know if you gave the murderer any cause for concern, but you would have cost me a sleepless night if *I'd* had you on my trail. I do so admire professionalism." She threw a shrewd, sidelong glance at her passenger. "I knew Dr. Kettle in the old days," she added. "Almost the first job I undertook after I qualified was the conveyancing of his house in Little Venice. Does he still have it?"

"Yes," said Tina. "I was to have had dinner with him there last night, but—but he had a heart attack and was taken away to hospital." To her alarm, she realized that her voice had broken on the last phrase and that she was very near to treacherous tears.

"Oh, I am sorry to hear that," said Janet Barden. And was too taken up with negotiating a tricky crossroads to comment further.

"Tell me more about the case we're on this morning," said Tina presently. "Is it going to blow up into a murder charge—as implied in your letter?"

"I don't know," replied the other. "Certainly, Dr. Davis was rather indiscreet, to remarry so soon after his wife died and left him a considerable fortune—and to his receptionist, who's twenty years younger than himself. It gave rise to a lot of speculation from the Nosey Parker curtain-twitching old women of both sexes who are his neighbours, and an outside chance for his dead wife's relations to claw back all or some of the legacy."

"What about the general practitioner who made out the death certificate?" asked Tina. "Is he coming this morning?"

"He died last summer," said Janet Barden. "I'm sorry I missed it out of my letter, but the thing was cobbled together in a hurry because the Home Office dropped news of the exhumation order in my lap at a moment's notice. And, really, that's the whole crux of the other side's case: the fact that old Dr. Newstock was over eighty and more than a little gaga. Implication being that he didn't spot the true cause of death."

"Are there suggestions of any other cause?" asked Tina.

"No. Except that, according to our client, his late wife was a tremendous lush. Could that help us—clinically?"

"Might do," said Tina. "Could provide an alternative cause of natural death. On the other hand, if the subject were a heavy drinker of strong spirits it would have made it easier to mask the taste of some poisons."

"Tell me, Doctor, is there any way that a mistake on the G.P.'s part—for instance, if he'd overlooked superficial signs of poison—might show up immediately upon examination of the body this morning? I have a special reason for asking."

"It's not really likely," replied Tina. "Yes, if it were something terribly obvious, like signs of asphyxiation, poisoning by mouth with a caustic liquid—things like that. But no qualified doctor, however old and past it, would ascribe such symptoms to natural causes."

"Then how long will it take to confirm Dr. Newstock's findings to the exclusion of every other possibility?"

"To exclude everything else—several days. Even if there is clear evidence of cerebral thrombosis, the search for other and possibly contributory causes will have to be pursued. The vital organs will have to be put to pretty exhaustive lab tests."

"How many days? A week—more?"

"Might be," admitted Tina.

"Oh! Those poor folks!" Janet Barden smacked the rim of the steering wheel with the palms of both hands. "They're going to go through hell during that time!"

Tina glanced at her companion in some surprise, for she

would not have thought that matter-of-fact and capable-looking woman would have allowed herself to get so emotionally involved in a case.

"You are convinced that there's no truth in the suspicion of homicide?" she asked.

"Yes," responded the other. "If Dr. Davis is guilty—if both of them were guilty—they'd have waited a year or so before they got married, instead of flying into each other's arms before the wife was cold in her grave. What some would call indecent haste suggests to me that they're innocent—it would never have occurred to them to be prudent. They didn't take into account what idle gossip, malice, jealousy, and sheer greed can set in motion."

There did not seem to be any reply to that.

Sawyer's Green Cemetery in the best of circumstances could scarcely have been a place of spiritual enlightenment; in the sluicing rain and under the dripping, dead-looking trees, with the green-streaked gravestones set like rows of rotten teeth around a semicircular drive and a factory hooter sounding off somewhere beyond the Victorian barracks of a hospital that stood just beyond the boundary wall, the place was a dreary monument to the impermanence of the human state, the friability of grief.

The heavy overcast rendered it still dusk, despite which a small huddle of rubberneckers were peering in through the railings towards the canvas screen which had been set up round a grave quite close to the road. As they drove in the gates to the beckoning of a police constable stationed there, Tina winced at the blinding glare of a flashbulb erupting close by her window, and she saw a young photographer, hatless in a seedy mack. With him was a young woman: dark-haired, with a hard, predatory expression; she ducked her head to get a better look at the two people in the car.

There were half a dozen other vehicles parked in the

drive adjacent to the screened grave, among them two police cars bearing winking blue lights. And a mortuary van.
Some distance apart from the rest, as if cast into the outer
darkness by reason of a grave sin, stood a small saloon with
a man and woman inside.

"That's Dr. and Mrs. Davis," murmured Janet Barden.
"I must go and have a word with them. Do please come
with me."

Tina followed her. The Davises did not get out of their
car, but the man accepted their proffered hands. While being introduced, Tina had the clear impression of two very
ordinary folk trapped in a situation which had slipped out
of their control. She detected no fear in either of their faces
—only the bland numbness of animals brought, uncomprehending, to slaughter, and had an impulse—instantly
quelled—to make some bright, reassuring remark. Taking
their leave, she and Janet Barden went over to join the
group by the grave. The Davises stayed where they were.

"If there was any guilt in them," said Janet Barden, "he
would never have brought her with him today. If it goes to
court," she added, "I shall try to get Marcus Struthers to
accept the brief. Of course—you know him, don't you?"

Tina nodded.

Warburton-Fosse, for all that he was a near-contemporary
of Johnny Kettle, looked a decade older. Nor did he wear
the burden of his years with ease; gawkily thin, pale-faced,
with a pinched, purplish nose, he could have passed for a
bronchial old vagabond. It was an image of which he was
painfully conscious, but which his every effort seemed only
to exacerbate, so that his expensive tweeds hung upon him
like the rags of a scarecrow, his tie looked as if it had been
tied with a spoon and fork, and his handmade shoes—totally unsuitable for a muddy graveside—were scuffed and
down at heel.

He had seen Tina May on TV and recognized her at once. "That feller Kettle's bit of skirt"—following upon Tina's recent successes in court and the media, this was how he privately referred to her. In the flesh she looked not half bad, he told himself, not that that lessened the folly of having a female blundering around in the essentially male province of forensic science. He brought himself to greet her civilly enough, without actually saying anything. The woman solicitor accompanying her he had met and crossed swords with before. A damned busybody.

"Well, now that the *ladies* have arrived, we might commence," he said to no one in particular. Whereupon the men from the cemeteries and parks department, who had already dug down to the coffin and threaded two canvas strops underneath it, hauled upon the ropes attached and lifted the mud-caked box with its tarnished metal plate bearing the name and dates of the inmate, while the teeming rain beat relentlessly upon the warped lid.

The coffin having been laid down at their feet, Warburton-Fosse treated Kettle's bit of skirt to an ingratiating smile that—he convinced himself—must surely have dispelled from her mind any suspicions that he might resent the intrusion of her presence—which he did. Savagely.

"I shall now repair to the hospital," he announced, "where they have prepared an examination room for me. Do I take it that you will be accompanying me, Doctor?"

"Yes," replied Tina, adding, "And I shall require a sample of all the tissues that you remove, Doctor, for independent testing in a laboratory of my own choosing." She said it quietly, but he was angrily aware of a note of authority in her voice, and the fact that she was well within her rights in no way lessened the affront.

"I will permit that," he snapped. "But it must be clearly understood that I am in charge of this autopsy, and no one else." He then strode off to his car.

On the way out of the cemetery gates, Tina and her companion were again subjected to flash photography from the same young man as before, and he was still accompanied by the dark-haired girl. The drive around the block to the gaunt and rambling hospital, whose clinical failures had down the years contributed a very large proportion of the cemetery's clientele, was a matter of minutes.

"How long will it take, the autopsy?" asked Janet Barden.

"Till about midday perhaps," replied Tina. "You're not coming in to watch, I suppose?"

"I've never been able to face it," confessed the other. "Dr. Davis will have to reidentify the body, of course, and I shall see him as far as the door, poor devil. Look—is there any way of arranging things so as to lessen the awfulness for him?"

"There are ways and means," said Tina. "I'll do what I can."

"Thanks. Look—I'll give you a ring after twelve for any news to pass on to the Davises. Shall you be at home?"

"Yes," said Tina. "Unless Warburton-Fosse spins it out just to demonstrate who's boss."

In the event, the autopsy was completed well before midday. The brain, which was in a remarkably good state of preservation, clearly revealed the presence of a massive thrombosis, thereby vindicating the late Dr. Newstock's opinion; Warburton-Fosse sliced on notwithstanding. Nor did he confide his theories and suspicions to Tina May, but dissected the entire corpse, removing enough specimens to fill a dozen jars. And Tina took for herself a sample of each for examination in a private—as opposed to the official police—laboratory. At the end of it, she and Warburton-Fosse bade each other a mutually frigid farewell and, he not offering her a lift back into central London (to her heartfelt relief), she rang for a taxi and was letting herself into No. 18 within an hour of leaving the hospital.

There were several pieces of mail for her. She was greatly intrigued by one that bore an armorial crest upon the flap of an expensively thick envelope which was addressed in a sprawled and showy hand.

Inside was a card:

Dr. May

Lady Miriam Struthers

at Home Saturday 12th

(frightfully short notice, but please do come)

R.S.V.P.

12, Vigo Court,

London, S.W. 3

cocktails 6:30 o'clock

Here was something, indeed. An invitation to cocktails with the Marcus Strutherses at their town house, and by the aristocratic hand of her whom Jeremy Cook had irrever-

ently referred to as "the bitch." Would she go? She thought
not. Despite the disclaimer, the thing smelt of an improvisa-
tion. Ten to one she had been invited in place of some unattached female who'd chucked at the last minute. Still, it
might be amusing to see Marcus Struthers—the poised and
forceful Q.C.—in his own habitat. And to meet his "bitch."

She tipped the card into a corner of the mirror over the
chimneypiece, in case (as she told herself) she changed her
mind before evening—and went to her study to phone the
hospital for news of Johnny.

The news continued to be good. No change. Sleeping
comfortably.

She was about to address herself to the rest of her mail
when there was a ring on the outside doorbell.

Jock back? The thought was first in her mind.

Surely not. And, anyhow, he must still have a key.

She went to open the door and found herself looking into
a face that was strongly familiar from somewhere close in
time and place: a dark-haired girl who was not alone; there
was a young man in a seedy mack standing behind her.

"Dr. May, I'm Monica Vane—of the *Sunday Courier*.
Hello." (The girl with the photographer at the cemetery—of
course!)

"Hello," said Tina. "What can I do for you?"

"Can we come in? This is Paddy Gorman, who takes the
pictures."

"Hi, Doc!"

Slightly bemused, she took the couple into her sitting
room and offered them medium-dry sherry, which was all
she had in the place. The photographer declined, but the
girl took a glass, drank it halfway down, and then produced
a notebook.

"I had in mind to do a depth piece on you, Doctor," she
said, head on one side, eyes crinkled at the corners and

looking very good-humoured and sincere. "A double-page spread for tomorrow. How does that grab you?"

"I—I'm overwhelmed," replied Tina. "But why me, pray?"

"Don't you realize," said Monica Vane, "that you have become a quite famous person?"

"I do not," confessed Tina. "And I must say I'm greatly surprised to hear it. Fame must be uncommonly easy to come by nowadays—a fact that has occurred to me from time to time," she added.

"Well, what do you say?" asked the girl, leaning forward and giving an added crinkle to the corners of her eyes.

"Provided you don't put words into my mouth that go against the code of professional conduct," said Tina, with good-humoured resignation. "But—honestly—what you're going to find to write about I just can't imagine."

"You leave that to me," responded the other. "Now—as to your background. Do you come of a medical family?"

"My father's brother was a vet," replied Tina, smiling.

"Very good," commented Monica Vane. "Vets are very 'in' nowadays." She paused, and without looking up added in a quite different tone of voice, "And you've been married." It was not a question.

"Yes, I've been married," replied Tina dully.

One might have known, she told herself. This girl's done her homework already, of course. Her paper will have dug out all the dirt on poor old Jock: his frequent starring appearances at Marlborough Street police court on charges of everything from "drunk and disorderly" to "common assault," through "passing cheques while knowing them to be worthless" to "attempting to obtain credit by false pretences."

"Your husband was—is—quite a character, so I believe," said Monica Vane, meeting her gaze.

"He describes himself as the Complete Renaissance

Man," replied Tina. "He's an author, you know, and an artist. They're not like us. Not like ordinary folk."

It went on, and she swiftly moved from the position of wishing that she had never agreed to the interview (and it was too late in the day for that) to the need to make some kind of defensive stance against the girl's probing questions.

After a while, her interrogator switched to another tack: "Do you think you're going to find the murderer—the Woman with Green Eyes?"

Tina nearly laughed aloud. "You shouldn't ask me that," she said. "That's a matter for the police. All I do is make a report on the state of the victims. It's left to the police to evaluate the forensic evidence."

The girl smiled at her. It was a nudging, all-girls-to-gether, we-know-the-score-don't-we? sort of smile. "Ah, but it was *you* who figured that the killings were all by the hand of the same person, wasn't it?" she declared. "You who coined the phrase"—she glanced down at her notebook— " 'the killer's signature' and 'as ineradicable as the nuances of one's handwriting.' I quote you direct, right off the video playback."

Tina had the sensation of being driven into a corner that she had no wish to occupy—simply because it was not her corner.

She said, "That was a perfectly natural and self-evident conclusion which any competent forensic scientist would have made. It's certainly nothing to write home about."

The girl treated her again to that irritating, conspiratorial smile. "Do you know what they're saying?" she asked. "In every saloon and public bar in the country . . ."

"Do tell me."

"They're saying that it will be Dr. Tina May who'll catch the Girl with Green Eyes."

Tina laughed. "How do they come to that conclusion?" she asked. "By gazing into their crystal balls?"

The girl looked affronted. "Never underestimate the opinion of the people," she said pontifically. "How do you suppose, Doctor, that the *Sunday Courier* got where it has, circulation-wise? By listening to and echoing the voice of the people—that's how."

There was no doubting her sincerity. Before that hard professionalism—misdirected though it doubtless was—Tina had no defence.

"I'm sure you know your own job better than I, Miss Vane," she said contritely.

The girl looked relaxed for the first time since the interview began. "So come on, then, Dr. May," she said. "Let the *Courier* into the secret. You've got a pretty good picture in your mind of what kind of person the killer is—right?"

"I . . ." began Tina, but was not permitted to finish.

"If you passed the killer in the street, maybe heard her voice in a crowded room, you'd be able to say to yourself, 'The Woman with Green Eyes is someone exactly like that.' Right? Right, Doctor?" She pointed accusingly.

"You've got it totally wrong," said Tina. "It isn't in my competence to . . ."

But it was no use. The girl seemed quite convinced that she was holding something back, something that she—Monica Vane—was going to winkle out of her and present to her readers. Tina continued to protest. Happily, she was let off the hook by the sound of the telephone bell ringing out in her adjacent study.

"Excuse me a moment," she said, rising.

"Sure."

It was Janet Barden. With a prompting of caution, Tina realized that she had neglected to shut the door.

"I was going to phone you," she said. "But I've got someone with me, and it slipped my mind."

Janet Barden very brightly got the point: "So you might

114

NO ESCAPE

be overheard," she said. "All right. I'll do the talking. You just give me the short answers, naming no names. Okay?"

"Fine. Shoot."

"Was it cerebral thrombosis, like Dr. Newstock said?"

"Yes. No doubt at all. Quite unmistakable."

"Good. Now, as to the rest—how long before the other factors can be ruled out?"

"The identification will almost certainly take a week. There's a lot of evidence to screen."

"What would you say is the chance of finding a secondary cause of death? From what you saw this morning. I know it's a lot to ask. You'll be reluctant to commit yourself, but it means one hell of a lot to the Davises. That poor woman's living on tranquilizers."

Tina thought for a few moments and said, "I think the tests will prove negative. That means the first identification stands."

"So we'll be able to close the case."

"You'll be able to close the case in about a week from now."

"That's great, Doctor. And thank you for your cooperation. *You're* great."

Tina laughed. "Thanks. I only hope that my hunch doesn't backfire and leave me with egg all over my face."

"I've got faith in you, my dear," responded the older woman. "It's an effect you have on most people, I shouldn't wonder."

"You're too kind. I'll send you my bill before next week, in case I'm proved wrong."

"No fear of that, I fancy. 'Bye, Dr. May."

" 'Bye." Tina rang off.

The photographer, Paddy Gorman, appeared to have been taking some shots of her sitting room while she'd been out, and Monica Vane was scanning the titles in her bookshelf—most of which were on pathology and the morbid sciences, along with her favourite humorous authors, such as P. G. Wodehouse, A. G. Macdonell, James Thurber. The journalist had in her hands the leather-bound presentation copy of her book, *The Future of Forensic Medicine,* which the publishers had given her.

The girl smiled. "I'd like for Paddy to take some pix of you, Doctor. And while Paddy's shooting, I'll fire a few more questions at you," said Monica Vane.

And so it was. She was shot in a variety of poses: reading her own book (with the title showing), speaking into the phone and tapping a pencil against her cheek, looking thoughtful with a lock of hair falling over her brow. And all the time, the Vane girl kept up a constant barrage of questions: easy questions on her background and family life, her professional relationship with Johnny Kettle, her hopes for the future and her career—that kind of thing. Nothing more about old Jock, or about the notorious case in which she was presently involved.

The photo session over, the last question having been asked, Monica Vane took her leave.

"Thanks for everything," she said. "Watch out for your piece in the *Courier* tomorrow."

"I'm afraid it will be rather thin gruel," vouchsafed Tina.

The other winked. "Doctor, it'll be a sensation!" she declared.

Which was all very puzzling to Tina May.

NINE

The young constable had searched the park and the woodland through, but had found no trace of the missing Darleen Underhill, aged eight, slightly built, brown hair, brown eyes, wearing a green mackintosh; neither alive and well and enjoying a bout of outdoor freedom, nor dead and in the state that he dreaded to find her. Neither did a special squad of police, brought down from central London in a motor coach, find any trace of the child, though they combed and combed again, till dawn, the tangled woodland above the park.

Meanwhile, through the night, the system was swinging into full action. Every known pervert and child molester in South London was brought in and interviewed, made to provide an alibi for the previous twenty-four hours and more. No fewer than three confessed to raping and murdering Darleen. They were instantly released, since all three were accustomed to doing this every time they were interrogated about a missing child. The more missing children, the better—these characters got their kicks at the confessionals.

In the police station to which he had been brought from a quiet game of pool at the Working Men's Club many hours previously, Gary Underhill, stepfather of Darleen, faced up to his third pair of interrogators that night: one a middle-aged detective, moustached; the other younger and thickset. Both in plain clothes, neither of them introduced themselves.

"What's your name, sir?" This from the older man.

"Christ! I gave that to the other geezers! How many *more* times?" Underhill was built like a wrestler, with a big man's self-confident aggressiveness.

"If you don't mind, we'll do it my way, sir," responded the other. "Your name, please?"

Underhill frowned in some puzzlement, as well he might. The previous pair had addressed him as "chum," "mate," and so forth, and offered him cigarettes. This new one—the one with the moustache—might have been wearing a bowler hat and carrying a rolled umbrella, he was so square.

"Gary Underhill." He spat it out.

"Address?"

He gave them that, and his family connections with wife and stepchild, and his occupation, which was that of motor mechanic.

"Can we go through the events of Thursday night, please?" said his interrogator. "It might be useful if you were to take a few notes as we go along, Sar'nt," he added as an aside to his colleague. "Start with your arrival home, Mr. Underhill."

"I got home for my tea about half-seven," said the other. "And the wife tells me that Darleen's in bed with the belly-ache."

"Was this an unusual occurrence?"

"A what?"

"Did Darleen's—er—bellyaches happen very often?"

" 'Bout the same as with all kids. Eats too many sickly sweets and chocolate."

"Did you go upstairs to see her, Mr. Underhill?"

The giant looked puzzled. "What for?" he asked.

"Why, to see how she was feeling. To kiss her good night, perhaps."

Underhill threw the moustached man a flat, uncomprehending stare. "The wife said she was asleep, din't she?"

he countered. "And anyhow, I was watching football on TV."

"Watching TV—I see." A few moments' pause, and then: "How do you get along with your stepdaughter, Mr. Underhill?"

A shrug. "Not too badly—considering."

The detective shuffled some papers and produced a buff-coloured sheet. "I see here," he said, "that last June, you were charged with an assault upon Darleen, in that you did break three of her ribs and knock out two front teeth. You were found guilty and given a six-month suspended sentence."

They were both staring at the big man. He dropped his gaze.

"It wasn't true," he said at length. "The clumsy kid fell over down the stairs and hit herself. I told 'em that. They wouldn't believe me."

"There was another complaint against you," said the other. "The Child Welfare Officer called at your house shortly after Christmas, examined Darleen, and found bruises on her back, shoulders, and buttocks. Also, she had a black eye. You denied causing the injuries. Do you stick to that, Mr. Underhill?"

"Yes. She was always getting into scrapes with kids in the streets. She can't help it in a way. They make fun of her, like."

"Because of her disability?" The detective referred to a another paper. "It says here that she suffers from retarded mental development and is educationally subnormal. Also, that she stammers badly. Is that why the other children make fun of her, Mr. Underhill?"

The big man bunched his massive fists together, kneading them each to each. "I 'spect so," he growled.

"Do you ever make fun of her, Underhill—or ill-treat her?"

It was the younger interrogator who threw the question, the thickset sergeant. Big he may have been, but the glare that Underhill threw at him, and the half-rising to the feet, made him reach out towards the alarm button secreted under the desk where he sat, one touch of which would have filled the room with shirt-sleeved trouble-shooters. There was no need for him to press the button: the giant subsided.

"I never did nuffin' to her!" he gritted. "Anybody who says I did is a bloody liar!"

After a while, the older interrogator said, "Right, Mr. Underhill, let's take the events of the afternoon in question. Give me an account of how you spent the time from, say, when you finished your midday meal till you arrived home. Take your time. No hurry . . ."

Wives, in law, may not be allowed to give evidence against their husbands in court; but there had been no preventing Gloria Underhill from sowing the seeds of suspicion in the minds of the law's custodians, nor were they to be blamed for acting upon it.

So, while the system was combing the district and beyond for what they might find of little Darleen, the interrogators leaned gently and patiently upon her stepfather; urging him to tell, again and again, how he had disported himself on the fateful afternoon of the child's disappearance; all their expertise and experience bent at detecting the slightest inconsistency—as if for a pinpoint in a dam, which, being further probed, can bring the whole edifice crumbling.

This they continued till dawn, till the time when Dr. Tina May was being driven to the cemetery in Sawyer's Green. They then gave Underhill a decent breakfast of eggs and bacon, bread and butter, and strong tea. He was refused a request to be allowed to see his wife alone, but was permitted to sleep the morning through in an unlocked cell. After a midday meal of sausage and mashed potatoes, bread and butter, and tea, another team went through the questions all over again. And so it continued.

Tina got through some paperwork in the afternoon, phoned the hospital for news of Johnny (his condition was unchanged), switched on the radio news, thumbed through a magazine, decided that she must really do something about her hair, got halfway through writing a letter to her cousin in Scarborough, and felt unaccountably put down when Alice—tarted up to the nines—popped her head in the door to say that she was going to the theatre with her current beau, the head of the science department at the school.

Tina was alone again in the silent house, and her eyes went, by easy stages, to the invitation card stuck into the corner of the mirror over the chimneypiece.

Half an hour later, dressed in a quite glamorous woollen knit with a tasselled shawl over her shoulders, she took a taxi to Lady Miriam's, which was at the other end of King's Road. It was only then she realized that she had been intending to go all along.

Just as she was ringing for admittance to the expensive-looking mews cottage in Vickers Court, Detective Chief Superintendent Alec Conigsby was boarding a train for Westhampton. Since the murder at Rowberrys, the trail of the Woman with Green Eyes seemed to have gone cold. He and Arkwright had sized up the situation and decided that the killer must be holed up somewhere, and that, given the random and apparently inexplicable nature of her crimes, all they could do was to wait till she showed herself again. Meanwhile, they had a handful of witnesses to attest identity when the moment came. The young fingerprint expert, working round the clock with his assistants, had found Eunice Shaw's prints on three of the empty cartons.

Conigsby declared that he was going to spend the rest of

the weekend at home, and he bade Arkwright to summon him if anything broke before Monday morning.

The main gaggle of the party was gathered in a large, open-plan room that occupied the greater part of the ground floor of the so-called cottage, which had once been a genuine cottage and the home of, say, a coachman and his family attached to the big house at the other side of the mews. Lady Miriam had acquired it as a town residence some eighteen months previously for around a quarter of a million pounds of her father the earl's money, and she used it as a pied-à-terre during shopping expeditions, theatre visits, the London season, and occasional parties. Whether or not for the reason that she mistrusted her husband and thought he might be tempted to use it as a place of assignation with *une amie,* she did not encourage him to stay alone in the cottage. "When darling Marc's in town on a protracted case," she explained to anyone who cared to listen, "he much prefers to put up at his club."

Tina May was admitted by the agency butler whom Lady Miriam always hired for the occasion, and translated out of the tiny hallway into the main room, where, beneath a ceiling that had been decorated by a young Mexican mural painter who was all the rage that year, half a hundred guests were engaged upon the elaborate and protracted social and mating displays that characterize the upper and upper middle classes in repose. It was quite clear, from the sheer numbers, that Tina had not been invited—as she had thought—to fill in for an odd, unattached female who had chucked.

"Dr. May! How *tremendously* gallant of you to come at such short notice!" Lady Miriam, trailing clouds of beige lace and expensive scent, drifted through the throng towards her. They shook hands. The other's palm was damp and Tina registered that she had a distinctly thyroid look about the eyes. "Come and meet someone," trilled her hostess. "This is Fiona Winn. This is Fiona's husband, Joshua. Say hello to the new TV rave, darlings. My charlady says that her dearest wish would be for her daughter to grow up looking and talking like Dr. Tina. Isn't that a too, too divine compliment, my dears?"

Lady Miriam, leading Tina by the hand, tripped over the hem of her elaborately lace-trimmed gown and would have fallen if Tina had not pulled her upright. The two of them met face to face, close. The expression of diabolical animosity that suddenly flashed in the other's slightly protuberant green eyes came as a considerable shock—as did the realization (the woman's breath reeked of alcohol lightly masked with peppermint) that she was more than slightly drunk.

And then the moment was past . . .

"Darling Dr. May, I'd like to introduce my daddy. Sweetie, I know you've been dying to meet the newest telly-box celebrity. My dear papa collects pretty women—and he simply adores *clever* pretty women. I'll leave you two together, though my poor mama, God rest her soul, was always careful never to leave him with the merest kitchen maid. See you later, darlings. Don't believe a word he says, my dear." She drifted away, waving to a newcomer as she went.

"Ripping little thing, isn't she?" The Earl of Wycherley was well known to newspaper readers by reputation. Thrice married and twice divorced, he had had a racketty career as an amateur steeplechase jockey (his licence had been withdrawn) and theatrical impresario (summoned and fined heavily for keeping a "disorderly house"), and had been blackballed by most reputable clubs in London. Raffishly dressed in a tight-waisted, hand-sewn striped suit, with Old Etonian tie, and a red silk handkerchief fluttering from the breast pocket like a pirate flag, he bent his expensively bronzed profile towards Tina and gazed unashamedly down her front. "And what do you do, little lady," he asked, "when you're not standing here and being charmed out of your mind by Nicky Wycherley?"

"Oh, I thought you knew about me, Lord Wycherley," replied Tina, amused. "I appeared once on television, for which I appear to have become poised in fame somewhere between the Queen and Guy the late gorilla."

Her companion was in no mood for light badinage, seeming to find it not conducive to his style of gallantry. Or he may have been a bit deaf. In any event, ignoring her remark, he inserted a forefinger into the neck of her frock, at the shoulder level, and slowly drew it downhill, trailing the fingertip along the line of her bra. "Call me Nicky, m'dear," he said. "I have a friend, a partner in one of my commercial enterprises, who produces video films for the cognoscenti. I wonder if you would like to star in one of our amusing little pieces? I shall direct, of course. Nothing to bring a blush to the damask cheek. *Honi soit qui mal y pense.* Taste is all."

"Tina!" Before she could respond to Lord Wycherley's fruity importunities, a hand was slipped in her arm and Jeremy Cook pecked her lightly on the cheek. " 'Scuse me, Nicky," he said. "I simply must introduce Tina to Pushpam. Be right back." So saying, and without waiting for a reply from the visibly miffed peer, he guided her away to another corner of the room.

"I'm a great one for rescuing damsels in distress," he said.

"This damsel is greatly obliged, sir," she replied.

"How are you, Tina?" he asked. "And did they not give you a drink?"

"I'm very well, thanks, Jeremy. And, no, they did not."

He hailed a passing waiter. There was dry martini cocktail and champagne cocktail. Tina chose the latter.

"And how are you, Jeremy?" she asked. "And where's Pushpam?"

He nodded glumly towards a group nearby, where a

ravishingly beautiful girl of Asiatic appearance in a gold-threaded tunic was being heavily squired by a posse of predatory-looking young men in patched jeans and combat jackets unbuttoned to the navel, most particularly by one of their number with a Vandyke beard.

"That's Pushpam," he said. "I brought her with me, but the Bar can't compete with boy-wonder movie directors."

"Poor Jeremy," she commiserated. "One will have to find you another nice girl."

"I've found me another nice girl," he responded.

"Dr. Tina! My *dear!* What have you done with my poor father?" Lady Miriam came up, a champagne glass in one hand, a martini in the other. And she was now distinctly weaving. "Don't tell me that you found his discourse too gamy? Not after all the japes you and the chaps get up to in the locker rooms at the morgue." She sniggered and took a sip of the martini, while those guests in the immediate vicinity ceased to chatter and tuned in to her ladyship's loud, upper-class bray.

"Mirrie dear," began Jeremy, extemporizing an interjection to deflect the drunk aristocrat from her intended prey, "I had luncheon with Bootles Wagstaffe today and he said . . ."

She waved him aside, not to be deflected. "Tell me, Dr. Tina," she said, "tell me about the high jinks you and the chaps get up to round the old mortuary slab, cutting and slicing away. What happens when you get to the rude bits?"

"I really have to be going," said Tina. "Just popped in to say hello. Good night, Jeremy. Good night, Lady Miriam. Thanks so much for inviting me to your lovely party."

Lady Miriam stared at her in mock dismay. "Oh, did I put my foot in it again?" she asked. "I am most awfully sorry. Never could come to terms with what George Bernard Shaw referred to as 'middle-class morality.' Do forgive."

"Come on, Mirrie." It was Marcus Struthers, the first time Tina had seen her host that evening. He took his wife firmly by the elbow and made to lead her away. "You really must circulate a little, darling. There are some folks over here dying to have a word with you."

"Let go of me, you . . ." Lady Miriam struggled with him, and tripped over her hem again in the process. By the time she had become righted, she appeared to have forgotten her play of taunting Tina and had joined a group over by the table.

Jeremy escorted Tina to the hallway, and Marcus Struthers joined them there. "I'm awfully sorry for the scene," he said. "My missus has been mixing her drinks, I'm afraid."

"It was nothing," said Tina. "But I really must go."

"Yes. By the way, our clerk had news on the grapevine that we may be offered a brief to defend a Dr. Davis on a murder charge, and I understand you're also concerned in the case. This is hardly the time or the place, but can you tell me anything more about it than just that bald fact? Maybe I can ring you tomorrow."

"The case will never be brought," said Tina. "At least, I hope not, since I've stuck my neck out to the extent of declaring that the doctor's wife died of natural causes as set out in the death certificate. If the results of the lab tests prove me wrong I'm going to wish I'd kept my opinion to myself."

"I see," said Marc Struthers, nodding. "Thanks for tipping me off." He took her proffered hand, and retained hold of it an instant too long.

"Such touching goodbyes!" Lady Miriam came up behind them. "How terribly, terribly cosy. Why don't you kiss her, Marc dah-ling? You know you're dying to kiss her—if you haven't already."

"Oh, for heaven's sake, Mirrie . . ." began Struthers.

"Did you know that he is *quite* besotted with you, Dr. Tina?" she slurred. "Positively drooled over you on the telly the other night. You're both much of a kind. Common as dirt . . ."

"Take Dr. May home, Jeremy," said Struthers.

"Oh, there's gallantry for you," mocked Lady Miriam. "So faithful Jeremy's taking her home? Well, I hope for your sake that he can be trusted not to pip you at the post." She collapsed in a paroxysm of laughter that only ended when the door closed behind Tina and Jeremy, and was taken over by an angry exchange between man and wife, in which her shrill invective blended dramatically with his angry diapason.

Clearly, the Struthers were in for another of "their nights."

It was only five or six minutes' drive from Vickers Court to Lochiel Street, but Jeremy, taking advantage of the one-way street system in that part of Chelsea, bent the rules and brought her home by what might be described as the "scenic route," taking in a sizeable stretch of the Embankment, where the lights of Battersea flickered on the surface of the fast-moving river. Outside No. 18, he cut the engine of his Lotus, leaned back in his seat, and regarded her.

"What a messy scene," he said. "That, at least, will cure you of socializing with Marc and his bitch as a twosome."

"How can she be so frightful to him?" mused Tina. "I suppose he's only reaping what he's sown. No—that was uncharitable of me. But did he marry her for Daddy's money?"

"I think not," responded Jeremy. "Neither for that nor for the dubious kudos attached to her hollow courtesy title. No, I gather it was she who called the shots and he simply fell for her, hook, line, and sinker.

"Marc, you see, was the archetypal barefoot boy who

pulled himself up by his bootstraps. Won scholarships right through to Oxford and the Bar. Was one of the youngest Queen's Counsel of his generation. Marked for high office right from the start. He had—and still has—the aura of promise and glitter that reduces old man Wycherley to his basic element—which is that of a drunken old porn merchant for whom the Queen would cross over to the other side of the street rather than be obliged to offer him the cut direct."

"Lady M. despises her father," said Tina. "She really detests that man."

"You're right," said Jeremy. "Very bright of you to spot it straight off. Not many do. And that, you see, is why she grabbed and married Marc—because, for all his poor background, he was—and still is—the brightest star that's ever blazed into her firmament. And for all that she cheats him rotten with anything in trousers that makes a pass at her, she hangs on to Marc like grim death, simply because he's the antidote to all the shame and humiliation that old Wycherley's brought upon her. She really works like a dog to push him ahead, and will never rest till he's Lord Chancellor and the Queen makes a point of coming up and talking to her at Ascot."

"And what does he think about that?" mused Tina.

"I dunno," confessed Jeremy. "He never talks about it to me."

"All very odd," observed Tina. "Good night, Jeremy, and thanks for the lift home." She pecked his cheek.

"Night, Tina," he said. "By the way, how's the Green-Eyed Woman case getting along?"

"Quiet at the moment, but it will inevitably hot up again without any warning," she said.

TEN

It is the proud boast of the proprietors of the *Sunday Courier* that the journal is not solely aimed at the intelligentsia, and at first glance this would appear to be true; indeed, on a second glance at the contents (made up of scandalous goings-on amongst the upper crust including speculations about members of the Royal Family, the private lives of show-biz multi-marrieds, revelations of sex murderers' wives, mothers, or girlfriends paid for on the barrel, half-page "glamour" shots of shirtless young women, and anything about cruelty to animals, to name but a few enlightening subjects), one is inclined to the opinion that the proprietors' claim is more than modest.

The paper had never been able to hold Tina May's interest for more than five minutes, even when coming across a discarded copy on, say, a long and boring train journey. Her surprise may be imagined when a *Courier* arrived unbidden on her doormat that Sunday morning, along with the usual couple of its more prestigious Fleet Street confrères. In fact, she had intended to ask her friendly neighbourhood news-agent to deliver one for that special occasion, but the matter had slipped her mind on Saturday afternoon. However, the banner-head announcement:

"I SHALL CATCH KILLER," SAYS DR. TINA
See Centre Pages

suggested a likely answer: that the newsagent, seeing it, had put a copy through her letterbox on his own initiative.

So it was that, after making herself a cup of coffee, and with the bells of the local parish church summoning the devout to Matins, she curled herself up in the kitchen armchair with that satisfying sense of self-gratification which comes to even the most levelheaded at such exhilarating moments, and opened at the middle spread to find out what the famous Tina May had been up to.

The cross-the-page heading was more specific than the "tease" on the cover:

"I SHALL CLOSE THE CASE IN A WEEK FROM NOW!"
TV "CORPSE DOCTOR'S" ASTONISHING CLAIM!
in an EXCLUSIVE Interview with
the *Courier*'s MONICA VANE

There was a picture of her reading her own book, another with the lock of hair falling over the brow, another that had been taken of her while leaving the Old Bailey after the Fawcett trial. And there was a head-and-shoulders of the redoubtable Monica Vane.

But it was the statement in the headline that disturbed her—that and the most unpleasant sobriquet "Corpse Doctor" . . .

Her coffee disregarded, she scanned the text, which was heavily paragraphed, divided up into blocks separated by rows of stars for easy reading, admirably terse and to the point, and signposted by eye-catching subtitles. Such as:

"My Ex—not like ordinary folk"

—which, of course, referred to poor Jock. On the whole, Monica Vane was merciful to Jock, touching only lightly upon his police court appearances, and even giving him the accolade of once having written a best seller—a pardonable exaggeration which had been put out at the time by his publisher.

The rest was pure hokum, and bore no more relationship

to the life and career of Tina May as she knew herself than
if it had been a potted biography of The Old Woman Who
Lived in a Shoe:

CINDERELLA STORY

Not quite rags-to-riches, the story of how this lovely girl of humble
origins (the only professional in the family was her uncle, a small-
town vet) rose to become a leading light in her gruesome calling
reads like a novel of our times.

Scholarship to an exclusive girls' public school. Scholarship to
Cambridge, where she avoided the social life and worked herself into
a nervous breakdown. Wrote, at 23, a book on Forensic Medicine
which has become a standard textbook in the profession. And rock-
etted to fame by exposing the wife-murderer Fawcett at the recent
Old Bailey trial. . . .

There was a lot more in similar vein. The Vane woman
touched upon her relationship with Johnny Kettle, implying, without actually shouting it from the rooftops, that
they were not only fellow professionals but bedmates. Tina
skipped over that part with disgust and came to the nub of
the article, which purported to be an account of the "exclusive interview" which the writer had had with "the corpse
doctor" on the previous day:

"I HAVE IDENTIFIED THE KILLER!"

That, give or take a word here or there, is the astonishing claim
which Dr. May made in my hearing yesterday. It appears that she
has arrived at her conclusion by a complicated method of screening
the forensic evidence—a method which she has herself devised.
Though Dr. May claims that there is no doubt at all, she told me
that it will be another week before she is able positively to NAME the
killer. . . .

In a coldly mounting fury, Tina read to the end of the
article, having done which, she checked the paper's phone
number from the editorial page and put through a call. To
her surprise, her hand that held the receiver was trembling

with angry indignation as she waited for someone to answer.

"*Sunday Courier*—editorial. Can I help you?"

"Put me through to Monica Vane, please."

"Who's calling her?"

"Tell her Tina May."

"I think she's expecting a ring from you." (Said with some amusement.)

Moments passed . . .

"Hello, Dr. May. Thought I'd hear from you. Just read the piece, have you? Like it?"

"Miss Vane," said Tina, now fully in control of her hands, as she had been in total control of everything else since that bizarre episode had burst in upon her life, "I am going to sue you and your appalling scandal rag for every penny piece the courts will allow me—which I shall then donate to my favourite charity. You will hear from my solicitors by the first postal delivery on Tuesday morning. Good-*bye!*"

"Hey! Hold on! Hold on, will you?"

"I've nothing more to say to you, Miss Vane. See you in court."

"Wait! Hell—what's your *beef?*"

"My—*beef?*" Tina nearly laughed out loud at the creature's effrontery, her rhino-like hide. "My beef—as you of all people scarcely need to enquire—is that a certain party talked her way into my home yesterday, and on the pretext of writing what she described as a 'depth piece' about me, produced for publication what amounts to a dangerous criminal libel."

"There was no libel." The girl's voice—it was scarcely believable—sounded smugly confident.

Puzzled, aghast, Tina did not then slam down the receiver; instead, she said, "Listen—you put words into my mouth that I never spoke. The basis of your rubbishy article was a claim that I made a false, boastful, and basically dangerous statement. If that isn't a criminal libel on your part, I've been reading the wrong newspapers and magazines!"

"All right, all right," said Monica Vane. "I concede that the reported remarks have been edited down and paraphrased here and there in the interests of presentation. Also, that they were not directly addressed to me. But say them you did, Dr. May. You said them, all right!"

"No! I did *not!*"

"You wanna hear? I taped your every word!"

There came a crackle on the line. And then a voice—her own voice—speaking disjointed phrases with gaps in between, as if some other party was carrying the burden of the other half of the dialogue, but out of earshot:

"Yes. No doubt at all. Quite unmistakable . . ."

Pause . . .

"The identification will almost certainly take a week. There's a lot of evidence to screen."

Pause . . .

"I think the tests will prove negative. That means the first identification stands."

Pause . . .

"You'll be able to close the case in about a week from now."

Pause . . .

"Thanks. I only hope that my hunch doesn't backfire and leave me with egg all over . . ."

"STOP!" shouted Tina May. "Turn that damned thing off!"

The recording crackled away to silence. Monica Vane came back on the line again. "Still denying that you said it, Doc?" she drawled. "Those were your very words."

"A private call over the phone!" cried Tina.

"Private—to Detective Chief Inspector Arkwright of the Yard, I guess. So what? I respected your professional status and didn't speculate on the identity of the other party to the conversation."

"You fool! You utter fool!" Tina closed her eyes in weariness. "You don't know—can't imagine—what trouble you've probably caused."

"You say I've caused trouble. Then tell me what trouble. Tell me! Give me the exclusive. Give me . . ."

Tina put down the phone on the other's rambling, self-seeking diatribe.

Alice came in soon after and found Tina sitting there, the cup of cold coffee still undrunk between her listless fingers. Alice, whose warmest wish was to live to see the overthrow of capitalism and the establishment of a worldwide state based upon the tenets of atheistic socialism as propounded by the lecherous old German whose hallowed remains lie in Highgate Cemetery, North London, was a regular churchgoer and communicant. She threw off her wet mackintosh and headscarf, shook out her tousled hair, and eyed her old friend and housemate warily, for though not a person of tremendous perception, she could see that something was the matter.

"Father Thompson was his usual unctuous self this morning," she said. "He spoke at great length upon the evils of self-indulgence—and he who's just bought himself a new motorcar. What's wrong, Tina love? Tell Auntie."

Tina told her, indicating the scrumpled copy of the *Sunday Courier,* which the other immediately scanned through and tossed aside with a snort of contempt.

"Well, what are you going to do about it?" she asked.

"Not a lot I can do," replied Tina. "They have the tape of me speaking over the phone and a good lawyer could make a perfect defence: a complete misunderstanding. With all their money, they have me on toast. Probably don't even care if they lost any case I might be crazy enough to bring against them. I'm more concerned about the effect this stupid article might have upon whatever plan of campaign the police have in hand at the moment. My name must be mud in Scotland Yard this morning. I've tried to speak to Mr. Arkwright, but he's not available."

"Well, there's no use sitting around moping," said Alice. "I'm going to fix myself my usual Sunday brunch. Whyn't you join me?"

"We-e-ll . . ."

"Grilled lamb chops, mushrooms, and new potatoes. A salad on the side. Followed by chocolate éclairs. And you can throw away your calorie counter."

She had the capacity to make Tina laugh. It had always been so, right from their school days together, when tomboy Alice, all scabby knees, had been the pride of the First Hockey XI and the clown of the Lower Sixth.

"Yes, please, Alice. That would be lovely," said Tina.

"Right. You lay the table and I'll get grilling."

It was a pity, thought Tina, that though they lived together in the same house, their paths so seldom crossed. Each with her own demanding job, different friends, different interests, their only real connecting link was the old days at school: the amiable bumble-bumble of mutual admiration and the eternal roundelays of "Do you remember when old So-and-so?" and "Wasn't it a scream when Miss Thingumajig?" and so forth.

With the lamb chops beginning to sizzle under the grill and the new potatoes boiling, they were at it again:

"Do you remember when we had the midnight feast on Clarice Stryker's seventeenth birthday?"

"And she'd smuggled in champagne!"

"We danced the tango, you and I."

"And fell over together. With you on top—and you weighed a ton in those days, Tina, sylph-like though you may be now."

"Alice, you hurt yourself rather badly, but were tremendously brave about it."

"Yes, wasn't I? And the scar stayed with me for years. How do you like your chops?"

"Brown on the outside, slightly pink inside."

"Then we're ready to eat."

"But—won't the potatoes still be rather hard?"

"Naaah! They're only babies. Sit down and pour the coffee while I serve."

"Black or white, Alice?"

And then the phone rang . . .

Scotland Yard? Their eyes met.

"I'll answer it," said Alice. And went.

She was back sooner than Tina would have believed. But it was not Scotland Yard that had summoned. By the defeated way she sagged against the doorjamb and gazed across at her with an ineffable sadness, Tina knew in the instant.

"It's—Johnny!" she said softly.

Alice said, "He's had another attack, and they think you should get right round there."

By a certain irony, the driver of her cab had a copy of the *Sunday Courier* tucked into the side of his door: she could see the headline plainly. And every so often on the way to the hospital, she saw him gazing reflectively at her in his rearview mirror, and hastily look away when their eyes met. She remembered having read somewhere that London taxi drivers are forbidden by law to spy on their passengers— and a short interlude to reflect on the ramifications of this odd fact (if, indeed, it was not of doubtful authenticity) provided her with a blessed pause from worrying about Johnny.

They crossed Lambeth Bridge. It was near here, in Victoria Tower gardens, that Johnny, who was an amateur painter, had set up his easel on such a Sunday morning as this and executed a very fine composition of the river with the Houses of Parliament occupying the left-hand side. She had brought him sandwiches, which they had shared. She still possessed the picture.

When they pulled into the hospital yard and she alighted to pay the cabby, he met her gaze. (Perhaps they were allowed to stare when the vehicle was brought to a halt and the brake on?)

" 'Scuse me askin', lady. But you are—*you*—" He indicated the copy of the *Sunday Courier.* "Aren't you?" He sounded anxious.

"Yes, I am me," she responded shamefacedly.

The door of the intensive-care unit was locked and bearing a notice that permitted only staff and near relations to ring and secure admission. A muted buzz brought a bright-eyed staff nurse. She was masked and smelling of antiseptic. She appeared to recognize Tina, and invited her to come in.

"Dr. Kettle's over there in the corner, Doctor," she whispered. "He seems quite comfortable now, poor old gentleman."

Johnny was lying under a sheet, with tubes sticking out all over him and electrodes connecting his tired brain with the encephalograph, which bleeped its own sad threnody for a departing spirit.

"I'll stay with him a while," said Tina.

"Yes, Doctor," said the nurse. "The consultant will be round soon. Would you like a cup of tea?"

How often, she thought, as she took a seat by the bedside and, taking one limp hand in hers, gazed down at the inert, noble countenance, how often has this scene been acted out? I've seen it so many times, but never played a leading role. The dying embers of a life. And always there's a little nurse who offers the bereaved-to-be a nice hot cup of tea.

She remembered the great forensic scientist who came to give a lecture to her group. Four—or was it five?—years ago. The magic, the almost theatrical flamboyance of the man on the podium, reaching out and communicating to his audience as he was later to enter the living rooms of half the nation through the medium of television. And afterwards, when the lecture was finished, and he was gathering up his slides and the few notes that he used, she had gone up to him. Shyly. He had seen the question hidden behind her lips. "So she thought she might like to be a pathologist, did she? Then why not put it to the trial? He had a call to investigate into a possible murder. Now. Tonight. If she liked, she could come along and hold his instrument case. His secretary was down with influenza. Could she take notes by cars' headlights?"

She thought she might.

A dark wood. Midnight. Police cars and blue-clad figures parting to allow the passage of the tall man and the girl at his elbow.

The revelation came in that long night, as he gently probed and murmured his findings and she scribbled her bastardized shorthand by the loom of the cars' headlights: how the long-dead, though far gone in benevolent putrefaction, have a dignity and a curious truth of their own. And it was this truth that the great pathologist sought and laid bare in the first flush of a summer's morn, with the dawn chorus of starlings and thrushes in the high treetops all round them. He met her gaze and smiled the oddly lopsided smile she was to come to know so well, and there was approval in the tired and red-rimmed eyes. "Had she written all that down? Good." It was not suicide, as the police had believed, but murder. And the great man had exposed a trail of clues that led straight to the killer.

The memory dissolved, and refocussed into another recollection that was interrupted by the arrival of the consul-

tant: a youngish heart specialist named Grant. He was un-
hurried, unflappable, businesslike, and Tina took to him at
once.

"Hello. You must be Dr. May. Liked you on the telly. I'm
sorry about him. Good chap. The carcinoma doesn't help a
lot. He's on heroin?"

"Quarter grain every night," said Tina. "I don't know
how much else. He never told me."

"Mmmm." Grant bent close to the patient, touched him
here and there. "I've put him on sulphinpyrazone for the
cardiac arrest, and I'll keep him on the heroin. Not the
world's best cocktail—but it scarcely matters now. The
heart failure will beat the carcinoma to it. I know which
way I'd want to go."

Tina murmured, "So does he."

"I sometimes envy you people for your particular discipline," said Grant.

"That's why I became a pathologist, Dr. Grant," she responded.

He hooked his stethoscope back into his pocket and took
her proffered hand. "Stay as long as you like," he said. "You
can only be of help. 'Bye."

" 'Bye, and thank you," she said. And was profoundly
grateful that he had not touched in any way upon entirely
spurious utterances of hope. They both knew the score.

Hours passed. She sat and watched over him, numbly
accepting from time to time the inevitable cups of nice hot
tea. "Business" in the intensive-care unit was brisk, as she
remembered from her hospital days it had always seemed to
be at the weekends, what with car accidents, family rows,
would-be suicides, and the like. Every half hour, she
checked his pulse and heart rate, monitored the drips. The
rest of the time, she simply sat and watched that fine Ro-
man profile and wished to get inside his head and share his
last thinking.

It happened around five o'clock. Something stirred just outside her consciousness. She jerked awake, suddenly self-reproachful for having nodded off.

Johnny's eyes were open, and his mouth was desperately trying to shape words. He was looking straight at her. The muscles and tendons of his throat were strained with effort, and his face was puce in colour.

"Johnny, oh, Johnny," she said, taking his hands in hers. "It's all right. It's all right."

"The answer . . ." he said.

"The answer—yes," she replied placatingly. "Rest, my dear. All the answers can wait till you feel stronger."

(Good God! That she should be trying that hoary old placebo on a death-chaser like old Johnny Kettle, who had twenty years in general practice before he ever reopened a grave.)

He seemed not to hear her. Working hard, he managed to mouth a word that sounded like "mentor."

"Mentor—yes, Johnny," she whispered.

Quite clearly, he then said, "Mentor. Look to your mentor, Tina."

He smiled, suddenly relieved. The awful dark discoloration faded from his face. "That's your answer," he whispered. And with a chortle, he added, "The Woman with Green Eyes. That's a laugh—a real laugh . . ."

His eyes closed. He sighed. And was sleeping peacefully, his breathing steady, heartbeats also.

Before Tina had time or opportunity to sort out the meaning—if any—of his puzzling statements, the intensive-care unit came alive with a banging of doors, the rush of many feet, the murmur of many voices. They brought in the victims of what transpired to have been a pile-up on the motorway: two men and a woman, all unconscious.

"Could I have the chair, please, Doctor?" The staff nurse looked harassed.

"Is there anything I can do to help?" asked Tina, handing the other her chair.

No, there was nothing she could do, thanks. Suddenly, Tina knew that they would prefer her space to her presence. Gathering up her things, she backed away from Johnny's bedside and the machine on the shelf above his head that bleeped and oscillated away its arcane record of the living force still housed within the naked figure beneath.

"Goodbye, Johnny," she whispered.

No one took the slightest notice of her going: they were all far too busy trying to save lives.

On the way home, she took a notebook from her bag and carefully wrote in it the disconnected statements that Johnny had seemed to regard as so vital. They did not add up to very much:

"The answer . . . Mentor . . . Look to my (or was it *your?) mentor . . . The Woman with Green Eyes . . . A laugh—a real laugh."*

My mentor—my experienced and trusted adviser—is Johnny himself. Then *why* must I look to him? And for *what?* And, for that matter, *where* must I look? The questions occupied her throughout the journey.

She let herself in, and found Alice on her hands and knees in the middle of the kitchen, ministering with prods and clucking sound and words of encouragement—to a cat of all things: a large ginger tabby of villainous mien, who approached a plate of scraps set there before him with a one pace forward, two paces backward step that was curiously reminiscent of some medieval country dance.

"Nice, pussy. Nice fishies for little kitty," purred Alice. "Eat, eat, you fat swine!" She looked up with a start to see Tina, whose entrance had passed unheard. "Oh, love! You're back. How's Johnny? How is he?"

"He's on the way out," replied Tina dully. "Just a matter of time—and not a long time at that. It's really a blessing."

Alice, who in all her life had never learned how to cope with other people's tears, said, "Let's both have a large sherry. What say?"

Tina nodded, and dabbed her nose. "Where did the cat come from?" she asked.

Alice, juggling with bottle and glasses, replied, "Didn't I tell you? He came round the evening you were on TV. Demanded a meal and departed without a word of thanks."

The object of their attention, making a sudden dart at the unattended plate, gobbled away the scraps upon it, blinked blandly up at the two women, turned on his tail, and minced ponderously over to scratch at the kitchen door. Alice let him out, and he departed without a backward glance.

"See what I mean?" she said. "He has to be a male, doesn't he? Cheers!" She raised her glass. "Here's to—Johnny."

"To Johnny," echoed Tina. *"And a quiet sleep and a sweet dream/When the long trick's over."*

"Did he recognize you, Tina?"

"He came to only once, and briefly. He said something which has to relate to a remark he made on the phone the day that I was to have had dinner with him, only he had the . . . attack."

"And what was that?"

"He said—" Tina frowned with the effort of recollection. "He said on the phone that he would outline a theory to me, that night, which was going to stand the Case of the Green-Eyed Woman on its ear. And, do you know, Alice? I've scarcely given it a thought till now, or, rather, till he said—*this . . ."* She handed her friend the notebook, open at the page bearing Johnny's message.

Alice pondered over it for a few moments. "He's the men-

tor, of course," she said. "And you must look for a clue in
something that he maybe once said . . ."

"Or published!" cried Tina, suddenly enlightened.

"That's a lot of books, isn't it?"

"No, it isn't, really. He wrote only two—and I have them
both." She leapt to her feet, swallowed down her sherry.

"Go to it, girl!" said Alice. "That's where you'll find your
answer, right enough. While you're doing it, I'll address
myself to thoughts of supper. Anything particular you
fancy, love?"

"I'm not at all hungry, Alice," said Tina, "but I'll attempt anything you put before me."

Her pathology "library" was set out in shelves by alphabeti-
cal order: *Anderson, W. A. D.* to *Wright, G. Payling,* and
included Johnny's treasured *Principles & Practices* (which
was a bible for all newcomers to the discipline) together
with his *The Illumination of Forensic Science.* The former
she knew almost entirely by rote, and it seemed an unpromising source for a fresh insight into the case in question.
Perhaps *The Illumination* might offer light in dark
places . . .

She took down the volume, opened it at the copious and
excellently chosen index, and worked her way through till,
reaching the main heading *Assault,* she began doggedly to
refer to the fifteen page references included under the sub-
heading—*by knife or sharp instrument,* in the course of
which she reintroduced herself to the classic cases of all
recorded times, from obscure Plantagenet and Tudor killings gleaned from manuscript accounts of long-forgotten
proceedings, to the Bennet case at Brighton in 1900, and
through Sienkiewicz's classic demonstration in Hamburg in
1913 to the notorious "Ripper" murders of the present decade; all told with Johnny Kettle's unwavering eye for the
potent detail and expressed in his limpid, spare prose style.

Drawing a blank with the *Assault* section, Tina, mindful of Johnny's declaration about the Woman with Green Eyes being a laugh, addressed herself to *Eye Colour,* in case something there might have some bearing upon that odd remark. She was lightly skimming over a set of rather dubious-looking statistics gathered by a Professor G. von Weissenfels in 1924 from inmates of the Breslau House of Criminal Correction, in which the Herr Professor related certain eye colours to specific crimes (Johnny's taste for the occasional bizarre would forever have excluded him from the rarefied heights of academism), when the street doorbell gave one long ring followed by another.

Tina was just getting to her feet when Alice came out of the kitchen. "Okay, I'll answer it," she called on her way past Tina's door.

Back to von Weissenfels. Or, rather, *à bas* von Weissenfels, whom—now she recalled—Johnny had claimed to have included in *The Illumination* for no other reason but to lampoon the Berlin school of statistical analysis applied to forensic science, and particularly to their asinine contention that a presumed high correlation between physical aggressiveness and lead-lined urban drinking water systems accounted for the excesses of the ancient Romans and others.

More on eye colour: Johnny's own long exposition on the coefficient of putrefaction of the eyeball and its bearing upon the loss of one very valuable means of identification was excellent—but not relevant to the present problem.

It was draughty. She looked round. What was Alice doing all this while at the front door? Why didn't she invite the caller in, rather than stand there with the door open and letting in the most unseasonably chill night air?

"Alice!" she called out.

No answer.

"Ali-i-i-ce!" More loudly.

Still no answer.

She got to her feet, crossed to the door, and went out into the passage. The light was on, and the front door an open void into the street beyond, illuminated only by the loom of the nearest lamp, which was on the corner. But no one standing there.

And then—she saw the crumpled form close by the door-mat, one arm outthrust and still gushing arterial blood from the wrist. There was blood everywhere: high on the egg-shell-blue walls, the elegantly moulded cornice, the cream ceiling. Two thick streams of it were snaking their way from Alice's twitching body and down the slight slope of the passageway towards her.

ELEVEN

Behind her closed eyes, and looking around inside her head, she tried to sort it out, and the task was made no easier by the two-toned note of the police siren, nor by the harsh, crackly voice constantly intruding over the car radio. What was more, Arkwright kept breaking in upon her thoughts . . .

"I've got to admit that I never thought this would happen," he said. "It's terrible—*terrible!*"

That was the key, thought Tina. It had never occurred to her, either, that the publishing of that ridiculous article—with its basic premise that she knew, and the police knew, to have been spectacularly false—would be dangerous in *that* sense.

"You had me worried when I read the piece in the paper," said Arkwright. "I thought you'd gone off your rocker—if you'll pardon the expression. Mr. Conigsby, he thought so too. Rang me from Westhampton and said, 'What's Dr. May think she's up to, pulling a gag like that in the gutter press? Isn't our job difficult enough without her going off half-cock and scaring the daylights out of the killer so that she goes even further underground?' And then we both thought it over, and we realized that you'd been misreported by Monica Vane, who's got about as much respect for the truth as the late, unlamented Dr. Goebbels. But, like I said, I never dreamed—neither of us ever dreamed—that it would bring the killer out of hiding to strike again in what she might think was self-defence."

(She came to silence me . . .)

"It's odds-on that the killer didn't know you shared the house. She'd think it was you standing there."

(With Alice fixing supper in the kitchen, it *would* have been me standing there—if I hadn't been so absorbed in Johnny's book. And because of that . . .)

"Even if she'd known you quite well, she could have made a mistake—with the hall light shining behind you, throwing you into silhouette."

(And because of that, Alice had to die most horribly!)

The police car slowed, and the motorcycle outriders slowed with it. They turned into the hospital gates, and the vehicle that came after them—the closed van containing tonight's victim of the Woman with Green Eyes—followed them in, and across the yard to the mortuary block.

She cleared the postmortem room of everyone. Of assistants, attendants, porters, police. Even of Arkwright and Conigsby (he had flown down from Westhampton by helicopter immediately upon receiving the news), and the two senior officers knew better than to argue with the flashing look in her eye, the peremptory tone with which she ordered them to get out, and stay out.

When they had gone, Tina addressed herself to a task of dedication. She alone it was who removed the blood-soaked rags of clothing from the body of her dead friend, laying bare the wounds now become, by repetition, so familiar to her.

There was no call for a formal postmortem this night. The killer's handiwork—signature—was plain to see. Her task she saw as more of a duty to the memory of a person whom she had known, liked, and admired, a person who stepped before the killer's knife in the place of her friend.

She must make good the damage as well as could be done. There should be no rough sutures—she must sew as fine a seam as ever she and Alice were taught on those far-off Thursday afternoons in the garden room of the old school, with the sounds of girls at netball coming through the open windows, and Matron's cat asleep in a patch of warm sunlight by the door.

Dry-eyed, she sewed with loving care, remarking to herself how—as happens after death—long-forgotten wounds will show up on the marble skin.

There, on the slender white leg, was the scar that Alice had taken during her fall on the night of Clarice Stryker's midnight birthday feast, when the two of them had together danced to the capricious rhythm of the tango.

They took her home again, and none of them broke in upon her thoughts again that night.

Already, the work of photographing and fingerprinting completed, special squads had cleaned away the blood.

Arkwright assigned two plainclothes detective constables to stay with her in the house. She showed them up to Alice's old room, where there was a single bed and a divan. All through the night and the day that followed, the two men kept armed watch. Unknown to Tina May, more armed police watched from the windows of an empty flat opposite, and her phone was tapped.

By a special dispensation from the Home Office, news of the latest murder was kept strictly under wraps; not a word of it was allowed to leak to Fleet Street, although it was noted by the phone-tappers that the *Courier* office rang Tina's number many times, and always in vain.

The new day dawned with rain that soon gave way to sunshine, so that the pretty girls and dashing lads of the King's Road were out in their summer clothes, and the window boxes in Lochiel Street lent that elegant old thoroughfare a bright new look. In No. 18, behind the locked and bolted murder door, Tina May remained a prisoner in her own home, and her whole day was taken up in reading, and rereading, every scrap of marginally relevant matter in both of Johnny Kettle's published works that might illuminate the theory about which he would now remain forever silent.

For one phone message, alone, had been accepted that morning: it was from the hospital to say that Dr. Kettle had died in the early hours.

Police Constable Dave Davis's beat took him from the junction with the London Road, straight up the High Street as far as the bottom end of the park, and back again to where he started from, only on the opposite side of the High. Ten minutes one way, ten minutes back; six round trips in a watch, give or take a bit of delay here and there, like directing the odd stranger or remonstrating with a jaywalker.

It was hot that Monday morning, and yet no orders had come through from Division to authorize shirt sleeves. Davis resigned himself to sweating, wriggled in his tunic to free his sticky armpits, tried to ignore the damp trickle that started somewhere up in his tall helmet, trailed past his collar and into the declivity of his backbone, till it was arrested by his belt.

Halfway down the High, close by Morris & Thwaites, drapers, a patrol car drew into the kerb nearby and his chum P.C. Frank Spargo waved to him. Spargo was in shirt sleeves, as the other noticed with a pang of envy.

"Glad you joined?"

"I'll bet!" responded Davis.

"See you for a pint afterwards?"

"Right."

Still cruising, man and car came to an intersection and both driver and walker looked left to cross. In doing so, both saw a young child—a girl of around seven or eight—in the act of filching an apple from the outside display of a fruit and vegetable store half a dozen doors down the street.

Davis walked quickly and quietly towards the small, un-suspecting culprit, and Spargo pulled round the corner after him.

"Hello, there—doing a bit of shopping for your mum?" The child looked round with a guilty start to see the tall figure in blue looming above her and grinning down. She was delicately built, had light brown unkempt hair, fright-ened eyes; wore a pair of scuffed jeans and a T-shirt—the standard juvenile rig. She also carried a bulging paper car-rier bag.

"What else have you got here, lass?" Two large hands relieved the child of her carrier bag. Inside was a young person's idea of a feast: it was stuffed with chocolate bars, fruit, cans of soft drinks, a tin of sardines, and bags of po-tato crisps.

"You do yourself well, love," said Davis, not unkindly. "Get a lot of spending money from your folks, do you?"

Still the child did not answer.

"Don't tell me you're going to eat all this," he said, with a mite more force.

"Su-some of it's for mu-my fu-fu-friend," came the reply.

Davis felt Spargo's hand take him by the elbow. The two friends' eyes met and held the same question.

Spargo squatted down beside the child and, holding her shoulders, said quietly, "Is your name Darleen Underhill, lass?"

A new fear flared in the girl's eyes. She made as if to slip from his grasp, but he kept hold of her.

"You and your friend like chockie bars and suchlike, eh, Darleen?" he asked.

She nodded vigorously, eyes brimming with tears.

"What's your friend's name, Darleen?"

"Du-don't nu-nu-know."

"Don't know?" He cocked an eye towards Davis. "Is she a little girl like you, Darleen?"

"A lu-lu-lady."

"A lady? Where is this lady now—your friend?"

"At the 'Lectric Pa-pa-pa . . ."

"The Electric Palace?"

The girl nodded.

"Let's go and find her, then, Darleen," said Spargo.

The owner of the greengrocery had been listening to all or most of the dialogue. As Spargo helped the child into the car, the man said, "Bloody kids! Can't drop your eyes for a minute before they're robbing you blind. Beat the hell out of 'em, that's what I say!"

Dave Davis thrust a coin into the speaker's hand. "Have this one on me, mate!" he said, with none of the fury that he felt.

The Electric Palace cinema was a hangover from the palmy days of the movies: an unlovely brick and concrete edifice off a side turning of the High Street, with a flight of steps leading up to dingy glass doors where in old times there always stood a commissionaire in the uniform of some Ruritanian admiral. An original bastion of the "talkies," the Palace had been the mecca of South-East London, to which stupefied thousands had flocked to see Jolson essay the first few faltering bars that heralded the greatest leap ahead in popular entertainment since Aeschylus and Euripides.

TV had brought the Palace to its present parlous state, where it was open from eleven in the morning till around the same time at night, seven days a week, and was a repository for all the outcasts and near-outcasts of the neighbourhood: the old pensioners, layabouts and drunks, the unemployed and unemployable—who, for a few pence, could win for themselves an all-day seat in which to watch—or sleep through—flickering reruns of the kind of movies that had been held in popular and critical contempt even in the long-gone days when they had been cobbled together.

To the Electric Palace came Constables Davis and Spargo, with the child Darlene Underhill between them. A word with the manager, who also worked the box office and sold ice cream during intervals (his wife operated the single projector), gave them admission to the balcony, where, with the little girl to guide them, they came upon, and woke up, a young woman slumped in the centre of the back row, with a seat next to her that was occupied only by a child's green mackintosh. A halfhearted chorus of protest issued from the patrons when the house lights went up in response to an instruction from the manager to his wife—but was immediately quenched when the feared arm of the law was espied.

"Just come along with us, miss," said Spargo quietly. He noticed that she had green eyes—but did not make the connection there and then.

Tina's two gaolers (she found it difficult to think of them as any other) were named Luke and Arthur; the latter was a cockney, the former from Belfast. By midmorning, she had got used to living with all the blinds and curtains drawn as if it were a house of mourning (as indeed it was), and accustomed to seeing her companions stiffen, become instantly alert, and reach for the weapons that lay concealed beneath their coats whenever a sound in the street outside—a backfiring car, the toot of a horn, running footsteps, almost anything—disturbed the tranquillity of off-King's Road Chelsea.

All morning she had been working on Johnny's books. Luke prepared a luncheon of ham and cheese salad, and with a nice sense of delicacy, brought hers into the privacy of her room. A tall, nice-looking fellow in his mid-twenties, and clearly susceptible to attractive blonde women, he seemed inclined to tarry a while.

"Still hard at it, I see," he said, nodding at the two

volumes on the table before her, together with a sheaf of scribbled notes.

"Yes, but I'm getting nowhere at all," Tina confessed. "You see, I'm trying to find a needle in a haystack, and the trouble is, I really don't know if, in fact, it is a needle, or even if the needle is in this particular haystack."

Luke nodded. "You're in trouble, Doctor," he said. At the door he paused. "That's a fine ginger tomcat you have," he said. "Puts me in mind of my Uncle Clarence, who'd eat and drink the house empty and dry, then be off without a word of thanks."

"I know the cat you mean," said Tina, "but he doesn't belong here. You shouldn't indulge him."

"Just you try telling *him* that, Doctor," said Luke.

Alone, nibbling unenthusiastically at a leaf of lettuce, she went over her last sheet of notes that related to Johnny's observations upon stab wounds generally, and of the ease by which death can be brought about by a sharp instrument directed by even the frailest of young girls—an argument which was most certainly supported by the murderous career of the Woman with Green Eyes.

She tossed the sheet aside.

Nothing there. The haystack forbore to yield up its needle. Perhaps she had, after all, been looking in the wrong haystack all the time.

And yet—Johnny had been quite specific: that I was to look to my mentor—i.e., to him.

But, then—was that exactly what he had said and meant?

"Look to your mentor"—that could equally well imply: "It is necessary that one—*not necessarily she, Tina*—should look to one's mentor."

Had he meant, then, that he, Johnny, should look—*or had already looked*—to his own mentor?

"SIENKIEWICZ!" She shouted the name aloud.

He was on the last library shelf next to Simpson, K., and

she railed at herself for not having thought of him before. Of *course!* L. K. Sienkiewicz had been Johnny's mentor and inspiration; had weaned him away from general practice and into pathology just as surely as Johnny, in his turn, had guided her faltering footsteps.

The answer to the riddle must be here. It *had* to be!

And it was . . .

Like the slow, noble unfolding of the last movement of some great symphony, the quest—which had so far been tantalizing and fickle, and in the end pointless—was suddenly taken by a sureness and predictability that possessed its own inner dynamic. The index contained a section under *Knife Wounds.* Hurriedly turning to the relevant page, she alighted upon a heading: *Some enquiry into the nature of wounding by sharp instrument.*

She read it through, and knew immediately that this was the passage to which Johnny had directed her.

It was nearly six when the first of the phone calls was allowed through to Tina's number. It was from New Scotland Yard. Arkwright was on the line.

"It's all over bar the shouting, Doctor. We've found her."

"You mean . . . ?"

"Yes. Green eyes and all. She was picked up on a routine check into what looked like a simple case of child abduction, and there it might have rested but for the fingerprint tally. She's our killer."

"Has she confessed yet?"

"Not a word out of her so far, but we're not forcing the pace at this stage. We've set up an identity parade. Four positive identity checks, and we have her whether she confesses or not. Like to come along?"

"Oh, yes, Chief Inspector. When—*when?*"

He sounded surprised, and rather amused, by the urgency of her tone. "Oh, anytime this evening," he said. "Just as soon as we've got all the witnesses assembled. I'll have a car bring you round."

"Mr. Arkwright—one thing—and it's vitally important."

"Yes, Doctor?"

"Do nothing till I arrive, please. Nothing!"

"As you say, Doctor." He sounded no longer amused. Rather huffy, in fact.

Woman Police Sergeant Jessica Fulbright was an ace stenographer, one of whose duties was to attend upon identity parades and take down anything that was said by any member of the assembled cast. The complex in which the operations took place was wired for amplified sound and closed-circuit TV, but one of the tapes ran out once, and since then it had been standard practice for a stenographer to double up, just in case.

W.P.S. Fulbright took her place along with the TV operators at around seven o'clock. Her seat was to one side of the auditorium, facing the three-way split screen, and close by one of the loudspeakers so that she could pick up every word, every sound. She had just made herself comfortable when the big shots entered and joined the lesser lights already assembled.

There was Mr. Arkwright, and the Detective Chief Superintendent from Westhampton who fancied himself so much, and no less a person than the Deputy Commissioner, who was talking earnestly to a woman she immediately recognized as Dr. Tina May. She looked rather pale and tense, but you could see that she was a real stunner.

After a bit of huffing and puffing—while the D.C. settled Dr. May in the seat beside him facing the screens—Arkwright faced the small audience and gave a sort of introduction, referring to notes on a clipboard:

"Ladies and gentlemen, the name of the suspect you are about to see is presumed to be Mary Lacey, Miss. I say presumed because she refuses to answer questions, even to confirm or deny that name, which appears on some letters found upon her.

"Bring in the suspect Lacey."

The young W.P.S. leaned forward in her seat as the TV screens flickered into life, revealing three separate viewpoints of a rectangular-shaped, totally unfurnished compartment with white painted walls, ceiling, and floor. A door opened, and in walked a uniformed police constable followed by a young woman in a blouse and skirt. She was accompanied by a woman sergeant well known to Jessica Fulbright as her friend Nan Tucker.

I don't believe it!—this was Jessica's instant reaction to her first sight of Mary Lacey, Miss. Of course, she knew that the subject of the parade was supposed to be none other than the mass murderess everyone called the Woman with Green Eyes; the fact hadn't been generally released around the place, but a surprising number of people were in the know. But that this frightened-looking little wisp of a thing could have slashed all those people to ribbons—the last one as recently as last night—was too much to believe.

"Bring in the non-suspects," intoned Arkwright.

They had come in from the streets, many of them politely importuned as they passed the very front entrance. All that was needed was that they should be of approximately the same age, height, and colouring as the suspect. And that allowed for a pretty wide margin.

"Form a line, please." This was from W.P.S. Nan Tucker, words which her friend duly dashed down in shorthand.

The women straggled into a rough line either side of the suspect, marshalled into place by Nan Tucker, who then addressed the object of the proceedings: "If you don't approve of your place in the lineup, you can change it now, or anytime you like. Give it some thought. Take your time."

The offer drew no response from the woman presumed to

be named Mary Lacey; nor did she look up and show any sign, but stared fixedly at a spot rather less than half her own height on the far wall.

A few minutes' silence. Some of the non-suspects shuffled their feet and looked uneasy. (And how more scared they'd be, thought Jessica Fulbright, if they'd been *told* who the woman in the lineup was believed to be!)

Addressing his audience, Arkwright then said, "The first witness, Norma Brown, aged twenty-two, unmarried, works as a kind of charge hand in Rowberrys storeroom, in which capacity she supervised the suspect, whom she knew—briefly, on the day of the Harlow murder—as Eunice Shaw. If she makes a positive identification, it can almost certainly be supported by at least half a dozen other people who were in contact with the suspect during her brief time there.

"Bring in the first witness."

Norma Brown was brought in by a W.P.C., who handed her over to Nan Tucker, who told the black girl what she must do. While this was going on, the eyes of the hidden onlookers were all upon the suspect, who had not moved in any way, but continued to stare numbly into the middle distance. And the image came to one, at least, of the on-lookers: *Like an animal brought to slaughter.*

Norma Brown walked slowly down the line, the W.P.S. at her elbow, the male constable remaining by the door. Nor could the black girl be faulted for skimping the task: she studied every face (and every face was a frightened face) and panned each woman from head to foot and back again before she moved on to the next.

When she came to the suspect, her reaction was immediate. Tapping the other on the shoulder, as she had been told to do, she declared aloud in a clear, high voice: "That's Eunice Shaw—that's her, right enough."

Jessica Fulbright wrote it down, and took note of the time of identification: 1914 hours—Positive.

Norma Brown was bustled hastily out of the compartment, with only one backward glance of regret towards the woman she might be thinking she had betrayed. The glance was not returned: the suspect had not acknowledged the girl's presence.

There was a noticeable stir of animation in the auditorium, and a certain amount of offering round and lighting of cigarettes.

"That was pretty conclusive, Arkwright," said the Deputy Commissioner.

"Yes, sir," responded the other. "And it's backed up with fingerprint evidence also. Ladies and gentlemen, the next witness is Norman Blakely, aged twenty-nine, unmarried, owns and operates a roadside snack bar a few miles from Coldshott Magna. This is in the area of the Westhampton constabulary, so I will give place to my senior colleague, and I hope I may say friend—Detective Chief Superintendent Alec Conigsby. It's all yours, Alec."

Conigsby got to his feet. "Thanks—er—Derek," he said. "To recapitulate: After the Westhampton killings, the suspect hitched a ride in a truck, assaulted and blinded the driver, and arrived at Blakely's snack bar early the following morning. That is the scenario as we see it.

"The woman known to Blakely as Ruth stayed in his employ till the afternoon of the following day, when, taking fright at the appearance of two of our police constables to whom she told a tissue of lies about herself, she then absconded."

"With the contents of the till, no doubt?" The interjection came from the D.C.

"Oddly enough, no, sir," replied Conigsby. "There was a little over two pounds in the till, but when Blakely went to empty it that evening, he found the money intact."

"She must have made off in a deuce of a hurry, eh?"

"Yes, sir."

Jessica Fulbright perceived that Conigsby's intent was to broaden out his small walking-on part to a big production, and she was wryly amused when his junior colleague and friend Arkwright seized upon the D.C.'s interruption to regain the floor and get things moving again.

"Thank you, Alec. Bring in the next witness."

Norman Blakely made an immediately good impression on the watchers. Neatly dressed, decent hair, clean shoes, an alert but not cocky manner, he went through the pre-scribed ritual speedily and with a minimum of fuss, halting in front of the suspect and laying a hand lightly upon her shoulder.

"This is the young lady I know as Ruth." And in a softer voice addressed to her: "I'm sorry, Ruth. I really am."

Pausing only to observe that Blakely's kindly words had done nothing to penetrate the woman's carapace of with-drawal, Jessica Fulbright noted them down in her book, together with the time. In the slight shuffling in seats and murmurings that followed the departure of the witness, she gave a glance towards Tina May. The pathologist took no part in the exchanges going on about her, but continued to stare fixedly at the screen that most favoured the green-eyed woman in close profile—almost as if she were searching for the answer to a question that occupied her entire concentra-tion, her whole being, to the exclusion of all else around her.

"I have to half apologize for the next two witnesses, who are only brought along here today because of the unique nature of their sightings," said Arkwright. "One of them claims to have seen the suspect leaving the staff doorway of Rowberrys shortly after the murder had taken place. The value of his testimony is lessened, you may think, by the fact that he shortly afterwards arrived at a nearby pub in a state of inebriation and was thrown out before closing time. However, for what he's worth, here is John William Walker, aged thirty-five. Unemployed and of no fixed address.

"Bring in the next witness."

Jessica noticed with some amusement that her friend Nan kept herself a couple of paces distant from the witness when she delivered her spiel to him, and it was not hard to imagine why. John William Walker looked like a tramp and probably smelt like a man who took no more than the occasional, enforced bath in some charity doss house. Tall, thin, pale, and wearing three-day stubble, he seemed to find it difficult to hold himself upright, and gazed at the policewoman with lacklustre eyes.

They set off down the line. Jessica glanced at her watch and speculated upon her chances of getting away in time to ring her fiancé and make an assignation for a late supper in the West End. Patting a side curl, she looked towards the screen that showed Nan and the tramp in half-length, back view. Nan had a really nice figure, there was no getting away from it. Being such a stickler for diet and exercise helped, of course.

And that tramp. Even if he did identify the suspect, who'd believe him in any courtroom? He was surely drunk right now. The way he was lurching. The way he . . .

Jessica leapt to her feet, her pencil and notebook falling unregarded. She opened her mouth to shout, but everyone was already shouting and on their feet.

The centre screen showed the tramp with his skinny forearm wrapped around Nan's throat, while his other hand was reaching out towards the suspect. The left-hand image was of a gaggle of terrified women—all with green eyes—hollering and backing away. The right screen showed the constable at the door diving forward to the rescue of his colleague.

The three cameras zoomed in on close-up simultaneously, to show Nan Tucker halfway to her knees, but gallantly grappling with her assailant, who, having taken her by the throat, was fumbling in his pocket. An instant later, he produced something that looked like a pocket comb sheathed in a plastic slipcase, which he raised on high above the suspect.

All this was faithfully recorded on videotape. For long after, the sequence was played over and over again, and the frames frozen at the split second when, a flash of steel being about to descend upon the upraised face of his intended victim, the assailant was struck across the shoulder by a descending truncheon; and again when he toppled, screaming with agony; and again to a close-up shot of the thing that looked like a pocket comb which had fallen from his hand.

It was, indeed, a metal comb. And the constable, retrieving it from the floor and failing to notice that the outer edge had been ground down to razor sharpness, suffered a badly cut finger and palm.

Form H.M.S.O. 693 (B) Metropolitan Police

/To Det.
Con. A.
Fellowes

*The Written Statement of Miss Mary Lacey, for-
merly of 16A Pryke Place, Nottingham. Given on
today's date.*

/Verified

I was a foundling and reared at the St. Mar-
garet's Convent Orphanage till aged 12 years,
when I was fostered out to Mrs. Annie Mosley,
a widow, of 16A Pryke Place, Nottingham.
Mrs. Mosley had her son at home but never at
school because of a mental problem.

Early on, Mrs. Mosley confided in me she
was worried as to what would happen to Ronald when she died because though very strong
and clever he could not be trusted out, so he
was always shut in at home. On two occasions
when he got out there was complaints from the
police of children being hurt and once there was
a visit from the R.S.P.C.A. as regards a cat that
had been cut up into pieces. I remember it was
on Ronald's 21st birthday and I would be 15
when Mrs. M. calls us both together and makes
me swear on the Holy Bible that in thanks for
her many kindnesses in bringing me up as her
own child I would look after her only son for
the rest of my life and not let harm come to him
nor let them take him away. Which I duly
swore. It was five years after when Mrs. M. died
and not a week passed before the police were
round with complaints about Ronald's behaviour, after which the people from the County
Asylum came and took Ronald away. I shall
never forget his words to me as he fought with
them.

He said, *"You broke the Holy Oath that you
made to my mother. If I have to wait all my life
I will come after you and give you what I gave
that cat."*

I do not think that the men who took him
away paid any attention to Ronald's words. But
I did.

/No
Trace in
Records

/Verified

/Court
Order
checked

/Continued . . .

Continuation sheet

(THE STATEMENT CONTINUES THE FOLLOWING DAY.)

It was last year and I was working in Bradford, Yorkshire, as a hairdresser's receptionist when I accidentally bumped into a girl named Clarice Springthorpe who knew me and the Mosleys in Nottingham. She said, "Did you know that Ronald is back home and as right as rain? Got himself a good job and everything. I'll tell him I saw you in Bradford." And though I told her please not to do that she must have because it was only a week after that my pussy cat was cut to pieces and put through the letterbox of my lodgings and I knew who had done it.

/At 19 Lossie St. /Verified

/Release Order H.O. No. 1667 (A) 15/ 226

(THERE FOLLOWS A RAMBLING AND IRRELEVANT RECORD OF LACEY'S DEPARTURE FROM BRADFORD, CONVINCED THAT MOSLEY WAS PURSUING HER. THIS ACCOUNT IS OMITTED HERE, BUT IS IN THE ATTACHED SCHEDULE.* THE NARRATIVE IS RESUMED WITH LACEY'S ARRIVAL IN WESTHAMPTON.)

(*Part IV)

/No record of Mosley's movements after this date, when he left his job

By the time I got to Westhampton the last of my savings had gone. I got myself work with a Mrs. Beverstock making lampshades and that's where my trouble really began. When I let slip I was from Nottingham, I knew I had to leave because I knew from the signs I had in Derby and Coventry that Ronald was following close behind me to get me. Then I got a lift to London, but the driver he tried to rape me but I struck out at him and escaped. Then I worked for Norman who was kind. But the police came, so I ran away again.

/For details of alleged incidents see Schedule, Part IV /See over . . .

/Continued . . .

Continuation sheet

/Abstract from psychiatrist's report. See Schedule, Part V	"IT IS CLEAR THAT THE SUBJECT'S OBSESSIVE FEAR OF THE POLICE STEMS FROM TWO SOURCES: (1) HER BELIEF THAT SHE WILL BE 'PUT AWAY' BECAUSE OF HER VIOLENT REACTION TO THE ATTEMPTED RAPE BY SUTTON. (Vide *Further Studies of Psychopathology in Everyday Life, Following Freud,* by D. K. Mattieu, pages 79 passim.) (2) HER CONVICTION OF MOSLEY'S ALMOST SUPERHUMAN POWERS, IN THAT HE WAS CAPABLE OF USING THE POLICE TO LEAD HIM TO HER. INDEED, THIS IS SUBSTANTIALLY WHAT HAPPENED."	
/Witness Tranter /Inquiries continue regarding cafe /A photo of Lacey was found amongst Mosley's effects. This he undoubtedly showed to both Beverstock and Harlow.	A lady gave me a lift in her car to London and I saw all these posters advertising jobs at Rowberrys, so I asked the way and got the job by using a forged card which I bought at a cafe with £5 from the money I earned at the stall. In the afternoon to my horror I saw Ronald Mosley queuing up for a job outside Miss Harlow's office, so I knew he'd seen the posters too and knew what I was about. So I ran again. I went by the tube train to a place called Peckham Rye and saw this TV programme in a cafe and how Ronald had killed all those people and I was being blamed for it. And I knew that he had trapped me at last and there was no escape. So I went and hid in a wood and waited for the police to find me. Or him to find me. Or both to find me.	/No trace of the party concerned

/Continued . . .

Continuation sheet

/Darleen Underhill. Missing Child Report No. 165/U/907

Then this little kiddie with the stutter finds me. She won't tell me her name but she says she's running away from her mum who beats her. We stay together. She's a great comfort. Nights we sleep in the wood. Days we hide in the cinema. And she gets food for us both. This goes on till the police come to me in the cinema.

(Signed)
Mary Lacey

TWELVE

Two days later, Dr. Tina May's presence was requested at a conference in New Scotland Yard. The summons, couched in the terms of an at-home party, was delivered by hand to No. 18, together with a copy of the written statement of Mary Lacey, which was marked *Confidential* and accompanied by a note setting out in specific detail the penalties under the Official Secrets Act for those transgressing its ordinances.

She arrived at the set hour of 10 A.M. and was met by a young officer, who immediately escorted her to a conference room on the fourth floor of the building, where a dozen or so people were standing, lolling, or sitting in groups around the perimeter of a large, oval-shaped boardroom table. She immediately recognized the Deputy Commissioner, Arkwright, and Conigsby, and was saluted by the latter pair.

"Glad you could make it, Doctor," said Arkwright. "This is just an informal get-together to tie up a few loose ends of the case. Dr. Heymans—he's the psychiatrist fellow, I expect you've heard of him—is going to enlighten us on a few points and will be with us presently, I hope. Would you care for a cup of coffee?"

The whole thing, which had the appearance of a coffee morning in some village institute, was metamorphosed by the Deputy Commissioner, who, after treating Tina to a stiff bow from the waist, addressed them all:

"Ladies and gentlemen, if you will please take your seats

we will commence the proceedings, with or without Dr. Heymans."

The seating was indicated by place cards. Tina found herself between Arkwright and a pretty, intense-looking woman police sergeant whom she presently recognized as the one who had conducted the memorable identity parade; an ugly weal under the woman's right eye bore testimony to that occasion.

The D.C. unfastened his pocket watch from its chain and laid it by his elbow. "This will not be a protracted meeting," he said. "To begin, I should like to extend thanks to Dr. May for putting to us the theory that the accused Mary Lacey might not, after all, be the murderer. It is a great pity that we were not able to build upon this theory, but there you are. One was not to guess, in one's wildest fancy, that the real killer would pursue his intended victim even here."

There was a murmur of approval, and Tina said, "Thank you, but I can't take credit for doing any more than calling Mr. Arkwright's attention to a paragraph from a book by the late Professor L. K. Sienkiewicz, and it was Dr. Kettle who pointed me towards it." She took from her briefcase a thick volume and, turning to a marked page, read aloud:

" 'In nearly all multiple stabbings that I have encountered,' says Sienkiewicz, 'a male killer, no matter how many times he has struck, has struck every time to kill. There is a *pattern,* an *intent,* in his blows. Conversely, I have observed that the female killer will almost invariably inflict a greater number of wounds, of which a relatively small number will —either by calculated intent or, more likely, at random—be fatal.'

"It was then I supposed," said Tina, "that the killer was more likely a man."

A silence followed, and Arkwright broke it: "We were lucky in that lineup," he said. "That animal might have turned loose on all those women with his blade. It's a blessing we had W.P.S. Tucker, our unarmed combat expert, on the spot." He nodded gravely towards the woman on Tina's right.

Nan Tucker shrugged. "I learned the hard way, that day, what any *real* expert will tell you, sir—a black belt's not much protection against a raving maniac with a knife."

The D.C. fidgetted in his seat. "Well, that's all water under the bridge now," he said. "I have reported to the Home Secretary that there was no possible way in which it could have been anticipated that the killer would attempt to claim his final victim here. Except that, in future"—he glared at Arkwright—"in like circumstances, anyone detected carrying metal will be required to leave it at the doors."

Arkwright seemed to be about to argue the point with his superior: indeed, was contemptuously muttering something about "metal pocket combs," when a new arrival was announced:

"Dr. Heymans, sir."

"So sorry I'm late. *So* sorry." The newcomer (who was known by sight and reputation to Tina), a stocky figure in a double-breasted suit with a white silk handkerchief fluttering from the top pocket, smiled puckishly at the W.P.C. who had escorted him there. "Thank you so very much, my dear. You've been *quite* invaluable."

"Your place is over there, Doctor," intoned the D.C. in the voice of a hanging judge. "We have just been congratulating Dr. May on her prescience in anticipating that Lacey was not the killer after all."

Dr. Heymans had a capacity to switch facial masks from comedy to tragedy at will. This he did. "Most prescient of her," he observed with a gravity that matched the D.C.'s. "But one would expect a scientist of Dr. May's intellect immediately to spot the Sienkiewicz Factor. That poor creature is quite incapable of sustained fury," he added.

"She was capable of clawing a man's eyes out!" growled Conigsby.

Heymans sank low in his chair, hands in trousers pockets, sulky-eyed; one had the impression that he did not much care to be challenged. "And look how she ran when she had done it," he said. "You may be assured, sir, that the guilt feelings stemming from her act were every bit as strong as the terror she had of Mosley."

"What's going to happen to her?" interposed Tina.

Arkwright answered her: "She'll be charged with grievous bodily harm and undoubtedly get off. The driver, who has a record for it as long as my arm, has already admitted to attempted rape. And she's got a good friend—more than a good friend—in Norman Blakely. He's promised to stand by her."

"Oh, I'm so glad," said Tina.

The D.C. glanced at his watch and tapped the tabletop. "This is all very interesting," he said, "but we are straying from the point. I have read your report, Dr. Heymans. Would you care to expand upon it a little, please? As regards the character of Ronald Mosley, I mean."

Heymans raised an eyebrow. "I would have thought," he said, "that my report set out the character of Ronald Mosley in definitive detail."

The D.C. was doggedly patient. "I'm sure, Doctor, that your report is perfectly understandable to a psychiatrist. But can you explain to us here present—in simple, layman's terms—how a creature who was never allowed near school, who spent the greater part of his formative years cocooned in his mother's house, was able to pursue this unfortunate woman nearly to her death, to cover his tracks halfway across the land, and almost dispatch his intended victim in plain view of the British police service—*and all unsuspected!*

"Dr. Heymans—what *is* Ronald Mosley?"

"A good question, sir," said Arkwright.

Heymans said, "In layman's terms, he is a compulsive homicidal maniac." He gave the D.C. a vulpine grin. "Next specific question."

"A madman—in the legal sense?"

"If a madman, a most erudite madman," said Heymans. "With an IQ of genius level. He learned to read and write from a child's picture book, afterwards graduating to a dog-eared set of Broadhurst's encyclopaedia, with the volumes C to D, N to P, and Q to R missing. He is thoroughly conversant with the Balkan Wars, the ballet, law and legislature, Britain and the United States, World Wars One and Two, and zoology. He is, however, significantly ignorant about Napoleon, psychiatry, and—surprisingly, considering his near-success—police procedure."

"What was in his mind when he killed all those innocent people, Doctor?" asked Tina.

"Surely—nothing!" This from Conigsby. "If he was as mad as Dr. Heymans says, he wouldn't know what he was doing. Wouldn't know the nature and quality of his acts—like the McNaghten Rules say."

Heymans shuddered and rolled his eyes. "The McNaghten Rules may or may not have been a useful yardstick in Anglo-American law since the mid-nineteenth century," he said, "but you have asked me here to give a practising psychiatrist's opinion, and I have to tell you that, in psychiatric circles, the McNaghten Rules have about as much validity as Santa Claus."

"You haven't answered Dr. May's question," said Arkwright.

"Very well," said Heymans. "To start at the beginning, he killed Mrs. Beverstock and the boy Finch after having enquired of them about Mary Lacey, having also seen the advertisement in the tobacconist's window."

"And he felt?"

"Deep satisfaction at having covered his tracks."

"What about Strong—the man who gave him a lift to London? The same?"

"The same. Satisfaction. Dead men tell no tales."

"Miss Harlow?"

"Same."

"And my friend Alice Wayne?" interposed Tina. "What would have been his feelings if he'd learned that he'd killed the wrong person?"

"Intense irritation at what he would have considered to be his own stupidity. And he would have been back again to silence you, dear lady."

Tina gave an involuntary shudder.

"It all adds up to this, then, Doctor," said Conigsby. "Psychiatry and psychology and all the rest—according to you, they're just bunk. A chap like Mosley—what you call in layman's terms a compulsive homicidal maniac—thinks just like the rest of us. He feels satisfaction, irritation at what he's done, knowing full well what he's done. Is that right—have I got it right?"

"No," said Heymans. And he was serious now. "The difference between Mosley and you—or me—is that his thought processes run along a single track that admits of no morality, no remorse, no conscience. Only self-gratification, self-aggrandizement.

"The process runs: I want, therefore I must have. This creature is in my way, therefore I must squash him. I am determined to kill this woman for what she did to me, anyone who tries to prevent me is on her side against me."

A long silence followed. The D.C. picked up his watch and reattached it to the chain that swagged across his lean stomach. "Is there any further business?" he asked.

There was much else. Another half an hour passed before the meeting broke up. But nothing else, no other detail of what was destined to go down in legal and forensic history

as the notorious Mosley murders, struck the same note as
Dr. Heymans's revealing statement about the nature of the
killer, which brought to Tina May's mind the old tag:
"There, but for the grace of God, go I!"

As they rose to leave, Conigsby and Arkwright sought
her out.

"If you're ever in Westhampton, look us up," said the
former. "My lads will always be glad to put out the red
carpet for Dr. Tina."

"I expect we'll be seeing plenty more of you at the Yard,"
said Arkwright. "And on TV."

"One thing I meant to ask," said Tina. "What's to happen to the little girl who befriended Mary Lacey—the one
who ran away from home because her mother ill-used her?"

"Some good came out of this case as far as the Underhill
family's concerned," replied Arkwright. "The mother tried
to give the impression that it was the stepfather who beat up
the child, and he loves his wife enough to let our people
think this is true. When Mrs. Underhill heard about this,
she went all to pieces. There's hope for her yet. And for
Darleen."

Dr. Heymans waylaid Tina at the door. "Can I offer you
a lift to civilization, dear lady?" he purred.

"Thank you, no, Doctor," she replied.

"I thought a luncheon together might be in order," he
said.

"I'm sorry, but I have to attend a funeral," she replied.

Heymans was quite put out. In all his long career as a
perennially middle-aged *boulevardier,* no person of the female persuasion had ever offered him that particular excuse.

Alice's mother's large family in Sunderland had ordained
that her remains should lie in their own mausoleum, and a
brother and sister had come down to collect her effects.

Tina had seen them off, and Alice with them, her coffin bearing Tina's wreath of arum lilies.

The day of Johnny Kettle's cremation coincided with Alice's interment, and there had really been no choice as to which ceremony Tina must attend: let Alice be laid to rest in the presence of her family; poor Johnny, whose only relation was a titled older brother—an unmarried misogynist with whom he had not exchanged a word or a letter since their mother's funeral—would be attended only by fellow professionals and members of the various learned societies to which he had belonged—if he did not have someone who had loved him to see him go.

Jeremy Cook drove her to the crematorium and made a guarded compliment about her mourning attire: a deep purple tweed suit and a black beret.

"But why Kensal Green, of all places?" he asked. "Is this out of oblique homage to G. K. Chesterton, Tina?"

"Bright of you to spot the reference," she replied. "It was a detail that both irritated Johnny and caused him a lot of time-wasting puzzlement: how he was going to be disposed of. The classic answer for one of our calling is to donate one's remains to a medical school, but Johnny was a tremendously private person and the notion was an anathema to him. I remember once"—and she smiled at the recollection—"he told me over dinner that he had decided upon a Viking funeral at sea. In the event, there was a note to me among his effects, and in it he instructed me to have him, as he put it, 'quietly incinerated at Kensal Green.' "

" 'Paradise by way of Kensal Green,' " quoted Jeremy. And observing in his rearview mirror that she was blinking away a tear, he said, "By the way, Marc's left his wife."

"Really? When did this happen?"

"The day after she made the scene at the party. Marc took his few things from the mews cottage and checked into the Savoy, leaving me the unenviable task of answering fre-

quent, frantic phone calls from Lady M. and telling her that
I had no idea of his whereabouts. Lies, all lies, of course."

"Has he left her for good?"

After a few moments' hesitation, he replied, "I really
don't know, Tina."

And there the conversation languished.

There were more people—mostly male—assembled at the
crematorium than Tina would have believed. As she might
have guessed, the TV people were there in force, along with
a camera team; clearly, the media was not intending to let
the notorious TV pathologist go out with a mere whimper.

She took Jeremy by the arm and filed into the chapel with
the rest, following the purple-draped coffin. The officiating
priest, an earnest-looking old man, performed his function
excellently well; he asked if there were any relations of the
deceased there present, and finding there were not, obviously amended his short address, which was on the subject
of bereavement, into more general terms.

And then, propelled by the discreet murmur of a hidden
machine, the brief, bland digression that Johnny Kettle had
planned for himself was over. She and Jeremy walked out of
the chapel into sudden sunlight, and Chesterton's verse that
her friend had added to the foot of his last letter seemed as
right as it had been intended:

> For there is good news yet to hear and fine things
> to be seen,
> Before we go to Paradise by way of Kensel Green.

EPILOGUE

A dubious spring of rain and a considerable amount of hail had given way to a promise of a rich, fat summer. The hand of summer was upon everything from the burgeoning trees to the lush grass that grew untended in Tina May's pocket-handkerchief-sized back garden.

Within a week of his checking into the Savoy, the gossip columnists' wild speculations concerning the split between Marcus Struthers and his wife had been fixed like a fly in amber by more sober announcements from Lady Miriam at Vickers Court to the effect that they were separated and seeking a divorce. This by chance happened on the same day that the homicidal maniac Mosley was committed to be confined at Her Majesty's Pleasure—a convenient legal fiction by which unfortunates of his sort may be shut up in criminal lunatic asylums till they die. Tina was summoned to be present at the proceedings, but was not in the event called upon to give evidence. Struthers, who appeared for the Crown, met her by chance on the way out of the court.

"Oh, hello. How are you?"

"How are you?"

He said, "I had news that the Davis case—the one that stood or fell on the autopsy report—is no case after all, and that you were right in your supposition that it was death by natural causes. It must be a great relief to you."

"More than I can possibly say." She was wearing a pale blue print dress: a summery thing that went admirably with the perfect weather. It seemed to him that she should be poised against a balustrade in the gardens of the Villa Cimbrone in Ravello, with the Gulf in its illimitable blueness far below her and the Mediterranean sky only partially occluded by the trailing vines that cast half a shadow over her loosely bound hair. Aphrodite. He tried the name again in his mind: Aphrodite.

She was looking at him questioningly; had probably made some remark that called for an answer.

"I must go," she said.

"Goodbye." He took her proffered hand. Then she was gone.

He told himself that it would have been entirely proper to have invited her to luncheon, or at least to a drink at the Savoy. Any other woman and he would not have had the slightest hesitation. Why, then, had he hesitated with Tina May?

She must, of course, have learned about the coming divorce. But, surely, that would not have prevented her from accepting a civil invitation. It was not as though there was the slightest truth in Mirrie's wild, slanderous gibes. A civilized person like Tina would realize that: would appreciate that he admired her greatly, that he was a man under considerable strain from a disastrous marriage that he was happily soon to terminate.

On balance—yes, he had been rather overprudent, but that was not a bad fault. Possibly later, after the divorce and whatever scandal the muckrakers of the press managed to dredge up as a by-product had been laid quietly to rest, he would give Tina a ring: invite her to some rather splendid affair where she would shine.

He strolled down the sunlit street: a tall, fine figure in legal black and grey. Passing a shop window, he observed his distinguished appearance and enjoyed it. He quietly mouthed a short litany which had carried him on his career from the slummy back street in Portsmouth to his present eminence:

"Mr. Marcus Struthers, Q.C.; Sir Marcus Struthers, Q.C.; Lord Struthers of Somewhere (not Portsmouth—not that!); The Right Honourable the Lord Struthers of Somewhere, and Lord High Chancellor of England . . ."

The divorce, muckraking or not, was prudent. That drunken lecher Wycherley, for all his money and position, was nothing but a drag to a man with ambition; and his foul-mouthed, shire-bred daughter likewise.

Altogether, Struthers felt so pleased with his prospects, present and future, that he bought a bunch of violets from an importuning gipsy girl who was lurking near the taxi rank, gave her handsome payment, and called her "my dear."

He left the violets in the cab.

It was then, and only then, that same hour, that Tina came home to 18 Lochiel Street for the first time for over a week; she had been living in a quiet hotel in the Bayswater Road till she felt strong enough to move back into the empty house with all its memories.

She opened the front door and walked in. A firm of contractors had repainted the hall and laid new carpets. The sun behind her streamed in through the open doorway and touched the unaccustomed newness, so that she felt emboldened to close the door upon the street and commit herself to the safety of her own home.

She walked through the house, touching things here and there, opening windows to let in the air, accepting everything she found, baulking at nothing, letting the memories well over her and wash away again like wavelets receding from a seashore.

The lock of the garden door was a mite stiff to open, for she and Alice had sadly neglected the small garden, and it had been out of the question, of course, to expect any help from poor old Jock.

As she stood there, planning in her mind an exquisitely formal miniature of Versailles, something brushed against her leg, and she looked down to see the monstrous ginger tomcat.

"You're out of luck today, puss," she said. "At least, I fancy so. But let's go and see." She walked through into the kitchen with the cat treading importantly at her heels.

There were two cans of sardines and one of anchovies in the cupboard—discounting other comestibles that one might consider not to be to the creature's taste. She opened one of the sardines—not the one in tomato sauce, but the one in olive oil. Leaving him then to tuck in (which he did with relish allied to a certain delicacy), she poured herself a small sherry and put on the stove the contents of a packet of curried prawns and rice which, according to the instructions, took eighteen minutes to prepare; curled herself, shoeless, in the comfortable cane armchair, sipped at the paper-dry wine, and let her thoughts drift.

The sherry was a present from Johnny; he had given it to her only a few days before the phone summons that took her to Number One Court at the Old Bailey, her meeting with Jeremy Cook and Marc Struthers; the beginning of a whole new chain of circumstances that had refashioned her life.

So very much had changed. Johnny gone. Alice gone. Jock gone.

Jeremy was some comfort, a good friend, a shoulder to lean on sometimes, but not too often, for that would be to exploit the gentle puppy-dog adoration that was really quite unsuited to his disposition.

Marc Struthers she instinctively did not trust, she decided. There had been something quite shifty in his attitude when they had met outside the courtroom just now. A man with a long way to go, and probably ruthless about the manner of his going. If one supped with him, one would need to sup with a long spoon . . .

The front doorbell rang.

Instantly, her gorge rose, and her heartbeats increased.

Be calm, she told herself. The devil is put away and will never, ever return again. You saw him with your own eyes being led out into the yard at the back of the court, bundled into the armoured van, and driven away through the crowds that had screeched for his neck.

Stepping over the cat and his works, she went to answer the door, only pausing on the way to meet the wide-eyed ginger stare that held a question.

"No, you may take your time over the last sardine, for there'll be no more for you. I don't run a restaurant for indigenous moggies. Don't bother to say thanks when you've finished. And there'll be a weekly account, payable in advance, by your plate next time you call."

She hesitated with her hand on the latch for only an instant before she opened the front door.

"It's Ruthin and Pryke, ma'am. Flowers for Dr. May."

Red roses! A dozen perfect and gorgeous red roses in a suave cellophane wrapping and a sash of contrasting silk. She signed the delivery form. But who could possibly have sent them?

"There's a personal note inside the envelope, ma'am."

"Thank you."

Back in the kitchen, she unwrapped the flowers and put them in a tall vase by the window. The thick, expensive-looking envelope was addressed to her—unbelievably—in Jock's sprawling, backward-sloping hand. She opened it up and returned to her cane armchair to read the note within:

Dear Tina, old girl,
I heard about the rotten luck of Alice's death, for which you have my deepest sympathy.

This is to let you know that you won't be troubled with "Old Jock" and all his problems anymore. I've met up with a v. interesting guy who has a scheme afoot that will almost certainly lead to Big Things. We depart for the Sudan on the midday flight today, which means that I'll be gone forever by the time you read this.

Good luck to you, dear. You deserve it.

Love,
Jock

P.S. Pity we made such a hash of everything. I accept that it was probably my fault that it didn't work out.

A tear for poor old Jock and perhaps for herself. They had been so young and ridiculously in love. Odd, that she should have seen his shortcomings so clearly with one eye, but have firmly closed the other against them, trusting that his very real talent would be enough to keep him busy and fulfilled. But there had always been the crock of gold at the end of the rainbow for Jock, always the "very interesting guy" to point the way.

But it had been so sweet of him to remember her on the day of his departure to the other end of the rainbow, and send her roses.

She replaced the letter in the envelope, for her drawer of memories and souvenirs. It was then that she saw the pencil scrawl on the back of the flap that some undoubtedly silly little shopgirl had forgotten to erase: *Charge to Dr. May's account.*

And with a sudden sense of release, the tears changed to laughter. A whole world opened up that was free of ancient associations, past glories, buried regrets. Dear old Jock—predictable to the end!

Between laughter and tears, she felt the cat rub up against her leg, and reached down to chuck him under the chin, upon which he leapt up onto her knee with a surprising agility for an animal of his weight and years. Very soon after, he was fast asleep.

Tina looked at the clock. Only five minutes and the prawn curry would have to be taken off before it turned into prawn mush and soggy rice.

Plenty of time. All the time in the world.

ABOUT THE AUTHOR

Sarah Kemp is the pen name of a woman who describes herself as being of "an interesting age." The daughter of an Irish peer, Ms. Kemp is a graduate of Trinity College, Dublin, and Cambridge University, where she read for the bar. Twice married, once widowed, and once divorced, she lives in a converted eighteenth-century watchtower on the Devon coast of England overlooking the approaches to the Atlantic. Two pug-dogs and a benevolent ghost share her seclusion.